"And One is for a mighty wish,
And so be Two and Three,
And she has left them to her son
And dived below the sea."

—*A Solatian Folksong*

The Magic Three Of Solatia

JANE YOLEN

Illustrated by Julia Noonan

ACE FANTASY BOOKS
NEW YORK

This Ace Fantasy Book contains the complete
text of the original hardcover edition.
It has been completely reset in a typeface
designed for easy reading, and was printed
from new film.

THE MAGIC THREE OF SOLATIA

An Ace Fantasy Book / published by arrangement with
Thomas Y. Crowell Company

PRINTING HISTORY
Thomas Y. Crowell edition / 1974
Tempo edition / July 1984
Ace edition / April 1985

ISBN: 0-441-51563-0

Ace Fantasy Books are published by The Berkley Publishing Group,
200 Madison Avenue, New York, New York 10016.
PRINTED IN THE UNITED STATES OF AMERICA

Contents

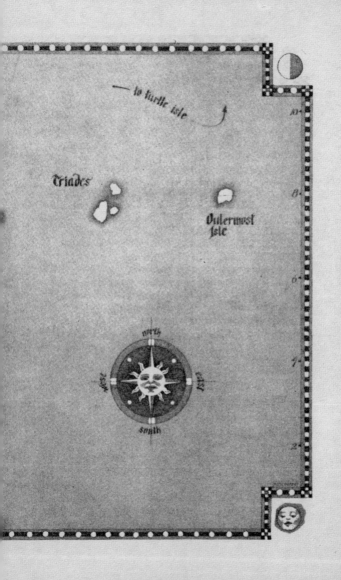

to turtle isle

Triades

Outermost
Isle

north

west · east

south

BOOK I

Sianna of the Song

Book I is for Heidi

Contents: Book I

Before

For more years than anyone can remember, the fisherfolk of Solatia have told this tale of Dread Mary. They tell it late at night before the hearth fires to warn their eager sons and daughters of the dangers that await them on the sea:

Once upon a maritime, when the world was filled with wishes the way the sea is filled with fishes, a witch named Dread Mary lived at the bottom of the ocean.

As she grew in size, she grew in wickedness. So fearsome did she become that no one—man or fish—dared oppose her will. And at last she was called ruler of the whole wide sea.

Even now no one dares go near the Outermost Isle, and especially Dread Mary's Cove. It is there that she dwells to this very day, beneath the tumbling waves.

Her home is a sunken galleon ringed with the bones of fishermen lost in storms. Dread Mary loves to rise on the midnight tides and sing the sailors down to the deeps in the windless, sunless sea.

She does not cry for the poor drowned men or their

widows alone on the land. Such sorrows do not touch
her sea-cold heart. She has but one passion, that witch
of the deep: for the buttons that shine on the dead
men's coats. And she carries the coats away to her
ship and cuts the buttons off one by one. And she
keeps the buttons in a barnacled box on the forecastle
of her home.

"Then why not wear buttonless jackets?" inquires some
quick-witted lad at the hearth fire each year.

"Tush, lad, and show our fear?" answers the storyteller
with a frown, and continues:

Every night Dread Mary runs her hands through the
buttons and sings this song:

> *No silver and jewels, but buttons for me,*
> *No silver and jewels, but buttons.*
> *Silver and jewels*
> *Are fine for fools,*
> *But buttons, oh buttons, oh buttons!*

So no one ventures to the Outermost Isle, though it is
less than a morning's sail from shore. And no one casts his
nets close to the liver-colored rock island, though the largest
fish shoal there.

And whenever a Solatian fishing boat sets sail, the fishermen carry with them shell buttons in a leather pouch.
When they are well out to sea, each fisherman throws a
handful of the buttons overboard and whispers Dread Mary's
name. It is called "buying the sea," for each man hopes that
the witch will take these tokens and leave him and his alone.

So it has been for more years than any Solatian can
remember.

1. Dread Mary

In the days when Solatia was a kingdom to be visited, the world was young. Mountains were newly green, having been thrust from the earth within the memory of the great-grandfathers of grandfathers.

In those days, the seawitch had been younger too. Her name had been Melinna then, a name compounded of beauty and song. The beauty was her own face, pale white with black eyes and hair. She loved to rise on the crest of waves and listen to the singers upon the shore, for she was the last of her kind, and lonely.

One of the singers was Solatia's young Prince Anggard, and for him Melinna had sloughed off her mermaid's tail and walked painfully upon the land. She had followed him up the hundred stone steps to his father's hall. There she had pressed upon him a jacket of woven seaweed. It was a jacket with three silver buttons that had come from the deeps of the sea.

"The buttons are magic," said Melinna. "Each can grant you a wish."

"I wish only that you leave me alone," replied Prince Anggard, and closed the castle door. But he took the jacket with him and never heard the rest.

"If twisted in just a special way," called Melinna through
the heavy oak door, "each button will grant a wish. But
only once, and only with consequences, and only if twisted
in a special way."

The prince never opened the door to Melinna again. He
had been too much in love with himself to return her love,
or anyone's love. So when he ascended the throne, he grew
old there with no queen beside him, nor children to carry
on his line. At last he died and left his kingdom to innu-
merable cousins who fought incessantly for the throne. And
the jacket with the magic buttons did not one of them any
good, for no one knew the real secret of the Magic Three,
as they were named and sung of in the kingdom. And at
last the seaweed jacket was worn by one of the cousin-kings
who was slain in yet another war for the throne. Years
passed, and the jacket had rotted like its wearer in the field.
Only the buttons and the bones of that king remained, the
silver no longer bright but crusted and lined with dirt and
debris.

When Melinna had been rejected by the prince, she re-
traced her way painfully down the stone steps to the strand.
There she found her mermaid tail and put it on again. Then
she dove back into the sea and swam beneath the waves to
the Outermost Isle, the last of the small islands that lay off
the Solatian shore, close but not too close to her lost love.

There, beyond the liver-colored rocks, in a cove that held
waves as gently as a cradle holds a child, she stayed, never
again venturing ashore. So she never knew that Prince Anggard remained unwed.

As the years went by in her watery home, Melinna grew
old, even for a mermaid, and a bit forgetful. She did not
remember how she had loved the prince with his beautiful
voice and his icy heart, and remembered only her gift of
love to him—the jacket with the three magic buttons.

After a few more years went by, she even forgot the jacket and remembered only the silver buttons.

Till at last all she remembered was how she loved buttons.

It was then that she started to sing the sailors down to their deaths in the cold, sunless sea. And soon the Solatians gave her a name that was as different from her old, lost, forgotten name as she herself was from the girl she once had been. The people called her Dread Mary, for they feared her more than they feared the sea. And they put up two fingers in front of their faces whenever her name was mentioned, to keep away "Dread Mary's Eye."

Now that kingdom by the sea, which had once been a place of laughter and love, was full of sorrow and fear. The wars of succession had raged for three hundred years, and no less than 113 different cousin-kings had claimed and lost the throne.

The kingdom had been called Solatia, after the sun, which always seemed to shine there with such power. Between the New Mountains to the south and the Northern Sea, Solatia had been long and low and flat, with crops green in the spring and gold in the fall. And prayers of thanksgiving had been sung there from one end of harvest to the other.

But the wars had ended all that. And many now called the kingdom Desolatia. Most farmers had become fisherfolk, reaping the hard-earned harvest of the sea. They remembered the peace of the farmland with longing every time a wave broke over their boats.

But all that remained in the once-green fields now were rusty swords, broken plowshares, and an occasional straying child.

2. Sianna

Sianna was such an occasional child. She was the daughter of Sian the button maker, a man of no faith but much talent. Golden-haired Sianna sang like a lark. Her childish voice was so sweet and clear and innocent that all the neighbors lovingly called her Sianna of the Song.

Young mothers begged her to sing their fretful babes to sleep. Old men taught her songs of their youth. And in the chapel, it was her voice that soared above all the rest when the Seven Psalms of Waking were sung.

But Sianna always went to the chapel alone, for her father would not go. He had lost his faith when he lost his wife, just six years after Sianna was born. She had gone down to her beloved seaside to gather the shells from which Sian made buttons. A wave as tall as a wall swept onto the shore. And before the eyes of all the men tending their nets and mending their lines, Sian's black-haired wife had been borne out to sea. "Gone to her kinfolk, gone to her rest," said the fishermen, for she had been one of their own, and they knew the power of the sea.

But Sian would not believe the worst. He was sure his

wife, his lithe-limbed wife, would swim home to him at last.

Weeks later, her blue vest, with its three silver buttons, was washed ashore. Only then did Sian accept her death as true. The jacket was stiff with salt, the buttons blackened by the water's touch. But Sian knew the jacket was hers. No one else in the kingdom had had silver buttons like those, for his wife had found them in the field behind their house.

The buttons were all that Sian and Sianna had to remind them of wife and mother. So when a neighbor woman offered to take the buttons and sew them on a jacket for the child, Sian gratefully accepted.

Every year, the buttons were sewn on a larger jacket for the growing girl. But they were never polished again. "Let me remember the cruel sea when I see them," said Sian, for he had been born of old farming stock and never trusted the waves.

His daughter, in her innocent wisdom, begged him to let her shine the buttons like new. "So we can renew our own lives," she said.

But Sian was firm. The black buttons, crusted with salt, remained the mute reminders of his wife's fate.

Sian was firm about one other thing. "You must promise me never to go down to the shore again," he told Sianna every day. He catechized her with the dangers of the deep. He tried to make her swear on the memory of her mother that she would not set foot on the strand.

But Sianna never swore such to him. Indeed she could not. Though she got her bright beauty from Sian, she belonged in her soul to her mother's fisherfolk kin. She could swim before she could walk, she could dive before she could talk. The sea fascinated her, it called to her, she felt it singing in her bones.

Still, as she would not hurt her father, she never spoke
of her passion for the sea. And if he remembered her early
ease in the water, he conveniently forgot it now.

But often Sianna would stop by the shore on her way
from school or run there when Sian was busy at work. She
never told him, so he never really knew.

Sianna waded in the tidal pools for periwinkles and starfish, which she dried in the sun and set on a shelf in a sea-
hollowed cave. She knew every sea creature by name, every
sea stone by sight, and every seaweed by its color and taste.
But she did not dare to bring any of her treasures or her
knowledge home.

If any of the village folk noticed Sianna at her sea play,
they did not tell Sian. For they loved both the man and the
girl more especially because of their loss. To betray the
girl's secret or hurt the button maker would have seemed
cruel to them.

And so it happened when she was twelve years old that
Sianna was down by the seashore gathering cockleshells and
sand tokens for her cave when a dark, ominous, twisting
cloud appeared far out at sea. It swirled around and about,
driving a giant wave before it as a shark drives a school of
pout.

As the wave ran before the twisting cloud, it grew in
height until it was taller than a wall and twice as thick.
Fingerlings were troubled to swim in its water and were
carried along by the force of the storm. And strangely, the
wave was silent—silent as the ocean's bottom, silent as
death in the sea.

One fisherman by chance looked up from his nets to see
the wave bearing down upon the village cove. He had time
for a single scream before the giant wave washed over them
all. Five fishermen and Sianna were carried out to sea by
the retreating wave.

The five strong fishermen managed to swim to shore,

heaving and panting and crying and touching the sand with their lips in thanks.

But Sianna was seen no more.

The grieving fisherfolk went to Sian's cottage to tell him of his newest loss. One widow woman, seeking to comfort him, brought the shells and sea blossoms that Sianna had kept in her cave.

But Sian threw the villagers out of his home, cast the shells out after them, and ripped the brittle petals from the blooms.

And in the year that followed, though Sian still went to the village to purchase flour and corn and wine, he never again ate a single thing that came out of the sea. He would stand on the shore and gaze out past the island chain for long moments without saying a word. Indeed, he never spoke to his neighbors again.

For Sian had taken a vow by the chapel door that he would never utter a sound until his daughter was returned to him from the sea—or until some real proof of her drowning was given to him. And so Sian the Silent became his name.

3. The Wave

But Sianna was not drowned. She floated like a sea creature on the crest of the wave. The spray crowned her head with jewel-like bubbles that sparkled in the sun.

Except for the jacket with the three buttons that she still held in her hand, Sianna was naked. The sea had snatched away all her clothes—her sandals, her dress, even the petticoats she had patched with care—and sent them below.

But Sianna did not feel any shame. For as she floated it came to her that she was a natural part of the wave. And no one had ever thought to clothe the creatures of the sea. She felt she was being reborn in the sea, reborn as a mermaid, reborn as a sister to the anemones and starfish that lived below the waves.

Sianna raised her face to the sky and droplets of water ran down her cheeks. She began to sing a song. She made up the words, though the tune was old. She could not think of any song that seemed quite right for the way she felt then—both old and new. She wanted a new song with an old tune to go with her special feeling. And she sang as she rocked on the top of the wave.

"I am the mighty wave, I flow
Where others do not dare, I go.
And all that's in the sea I know.
I am the wave.

I am the mighty wave, I grow
Encompassing all things below
Into my restless undertow
I am the wave.

While other things move to and fro,
It seems that I must ceaseless flow
In just one way—it is not so.
I am the wave.

For like all life, my motions go
In all directions as I grow,
And like all life, I ceaseless flow.
I am the wave."

Sianna felt so totally new and at one with the sea that she almost tossed the jacket with the buttons into the trough of the wave. But a sudden painful memory of her father, weak and dry on the shore, stayed her hand. And because she cherished the jacket for his sake and not her own, she kept it.

The wave continued to roll on, past the Inner Islands, the Mean Isles, the group of three called the Triades, till it came close to the Outermost Isle. But Sianna felt only elation. It was not in her then to feel fear. And she sat on top of the wave like a queen upon a throne.

Thus feeling her new power, Sianna decided to lie face down in the water and watch the sea creatures that were caught in the tow. But she underestimated the strength of the mighty wave. Before she could even struggle, it had

sucked her down, down, down into the deeps. With her
eyes wide open and her mouth in a bubbly scream, Sianna
was drawn down to the ocean floor. Her long golden hair
streamed out behind her as she fell, and she looked like
some exotic mer-creature in a dive.

She landed by the side of a sunken galleon. She lay there
white as bleached bone, her hair spread around her like rare
cloth. Little spotted fish circled her where she lay, still and
unbreathing, water within and water without, the jacket
clutched in her hand.

From the forecastle of the sunken ship, Dread Mary had
watched Sianna's descent. And when the girl had cascaded
to the ocean floor, Mary swam over, her fishtail making
scant murmurs in the sea. She seized the jacket with its
three blackened prizes and started back. But the gleam of
Sianna's hair, golden even under the sea, made her pause.

Some instinct, which she afterward could not have explained, made Dread Mary turn back. Lifting the girl in her
arms, skin against skin, she rose up on the tide. When the
two broke through the surface, the girl gave a frothy gasp
and began to cough. She half-turned in Dread Mary's arms
and reached out for her.

"Mother?" she asked, for it seemed to her that she was
a child again in her dark-haired mother's arms.

"Tush, child," said the witch of the sea as she swam
with her precious burden toward the cove.

4. The Outermost Isle

Sianna did not wake again during the ride to the shore. And when the seawitch put the girl down on the beach, she knelt on her fishtail, half in and half out of the sea, and sucked the rest of the water from the girl's lungs. Then casting a backward glance at the sleeping Sianna, the seawitch dove back into the sea.

Sianna slept all through the afternoon, through moonrise and moonset, and into the dawn. The soft winds dried her and kept her warm. But in the morning she awoke, stiff with sleep, and looked about.

Then she noticed she was naked and nearly wept with shame. She glanced around quickly and saw no one either up the beach or down. So she rose cautiously to her knees, then stood and stretched her arms and legs. As no one was about, the feeling of shame left her. She began to spin around and around. Her hair in bright tangles spun out from her head like a golden web.

She gave a mighty shout that echoed from the grove of trees encroaching on the beach. It was a shout of thanksgiving, of being alive.

There was no answer but a bird song.

Sianna whistled in return and a strange golden lark flew out of the wood. It circled three times around her head, then settled down in the sand quite near her feet.

"Why," said Sianna, so surprised she spoke aloud, "it is the *Gard-lann*, the king-lark. I thought they were no more."

As if answering, the lark whistled.

"Well, little golden bird, here we are," said Sianna. "But where are we?"

The golden lark cocked its head to one side as if considering the question. *"Sia, sia, sia,"* it said.

Sianna turned and stood on tiptoe, peering out to the nearest islands. "Those three must be the Triades," she said, partly to herself, partly to the bird. "And farther on, those ridges that stretch out in a line must be the Mean Isles. Don't you think so?"

The bird whistled again as if in encouragement.

"Which means," said Sianna, and she lay down and with her finger drew a strange configuration in the sand, "Triades thus, Means thus, and I am . . ." Here she plunged her thumb deeply into the sand. "On the Outermost Isle!"

It seemed that once she said it, it was suddenly true. What she had guessed at before took on a horrifying reality as soon as it was named. Unbidden, tears came to her eyes and began to trickle down the sides of her nose.

"I wonder if Dread Mary *does* live hereabouts?" she asked herself. "I wonder if she really does collect buttons?" And then she shouted, *"Buttons!"*

Sianna twisted around violently, but she could not find her jacket. She jumped to her feet and ran up and down the beach, peering out toward the sea as if to discover the jacket snagged on a piece of driftwood.

For fully half the day she ran around the beach of the Outermost Isle, circling it many times in her search. It was a small islet, with a wood grove that held no beasts but a few golden butterflies and the golden lark. The cove was little more than a groove in the otherwise oval of the isle. And nowhere was the jacket to be seen.

By the time she was fully convinced the jacket was gone forever, Sianna was ravenous. Her next trip around the island was more for food than for the jacket with her mother's treasured buttons. But she did not recognize the seaweeds that grew in the tidal pools. They were as strange and different as if they had been transported from another world. She was afraid that to eat them might mean her death—and equally afraid of death from not eating at all. She even tried to grub beneath a rock for worms or bugs, like a little beast of the field. But the three small crawlers she found were so unappetizing that she threw herself down in a fit of tears and for the first time surrendered herself to despair and exhaustion. She remained on the beach alternately weeping and napping till the moon rose over the horizon.

She went to sleep then, in the moon's light. She was beginning to feel the cold.

5. The Coral House

When Sianna awoke she was lying on a cold floor in a darkened house. Light barely peeked through a window that was hung with a seaweed curtain. A small shaft of the light had passed over her eyes, and it was that which had awakened her.

Sianna looked around in terror. It was like no house she had ever seen. She remembered the wave. She remembered her many trips around the island. She remembered her despairing search for food. But somehow this was the most terrifying of all.

She got up and ran to the door. It was made from two pieces of wood that looked as though they might have been hatch covers that had long lain under the sea. They weren't locked, she noted gratefully.

Cautiously, Sianna opened the top part of the door. There was no one there. But the smell of food was in the air.

"Food?" she asked herself. Then, "Food!" she shouted. Without another thought for caution or fear, she flung open the bottom part of the door. There in front of the house was a large mollusk shell filled with cooked sea plants and the speckled eggs of some seabird. A coral cup was filled with what was certainly berry wine.

Sianna threw herself down on the sand and ate the food with her fingers. After she finished the last drop of drink and the last morsel of food, she remembered to say grace. She changed it to suit the occasion.

"For these gifts which I have just received," she said with great fervor, "I thank thee."

But she was not sure who it was she was really thanking. There were dainty human footprints that led up to the dish from the sea, and the same footprints all around the coral house. But they all led back to a strange depression at the edge of the sea. It was as if some great sea creature had lain on the beach and disgorged a good fairy to care for her.

Was it magic? Or was it—and she could not believe it to be true—Dread Mary? For if it had been Dread Mary's doings, surely Sianna would now be dead, drowned, and bleached to the bone, a decoration for the witch's galleon. At least that was how the story went. Sianna remembered the old storyteller saying just a few days past, "The galleon is ringed with the bones of fishermen lost in storms."

It was surely a puzzle. But try as she might, Sianna could not put an answer to it. So she went instead to investigate the coral house.

It was not entirely coral, that she saw at once. Tiger cowries outlined the single window. An arch of scallops was over the door. At least, she thought with grim satisfaction, she recognized the shells. The roof was slanted and spiked at each corner with some kind of giant conch. And the floor was a mosaic of the sea, fishes and eels, sharks and seals, and even a mermaid drifting along in one corner. Sianna had to lift the strands of seaweed on the window and open wide both parts of the door to let in enough light to see it. And when she looked even more carefully, she saw that it was all done with pieces of clam shells.

"It must be magic," Sianna said. "Or else a miracle."

But believing in magic and miracles did not mean she should not also help herself. She had been well used to that at home since she had had to be a mother to herself.

Home! The word caught strangely in her mind. She had almost forgotten home. She knelt down in the sand and in a trembling voice sang a song of thanksgiving for her safe arrival and another, a prayer, for her safe return home. Her pure voice rang out over the tiny isle, echoing in the stillness. Out in the cove the water trembled ever so slightly as if sea ears were listening under the waves.

Sianna finished her song and stood up. She picked up the mollusk plate and coral cup and carried them down to the water's edge, where she washed them with care. She placed them beside the little house and set out again around the isle.

This time she went slowly and with deliberation, not anxiously and with fear. She began to see familiar places: there a path through the wood, there the rock she had overturned looking for worms, there a bird's nest that must belong to the golden lark. And there again, the coral house.

Coming on the house from the other side, she was struck by its simplicity. And what had at first seemed magic now seemed reasonable when viewed with calm. Such a house might be set up in a single night. Why, she herself could do it, except perhaps for the marvelous floor.

On the way around the second time, Sianna discovered a large piece of driftwood she had not noticed before. It was heavy, but she was able to drag it slowly behind her all the way to the house. Above her head, the golden lark circled and scolded as if to show the way.

Sianna thought the wood might do as a table. Though it was low, it had three stubby legs, and if she sat in the sand, it was just the right height. She moved it next to the house and set the cup and plate upon it. Then she sat down and began to wait for her unknown friend.

"At least," she thought, "I can thank whomever—or whatever—myself."

But the sun moved slowly across the sky and no one came. Only a few fish leaped far out at sea. And once Sianna thought she saw the spouting of a whale.

She was beginning to get hungry again. But she was sleepier still. And so, head on hands, hands on the table, Sianna at last fell into a sleep. She dreamed she was home making silver buttons out of the bones of fish she had caught swimming about in her father's shop.

6. A Night of Watching

When Sianna woke up on her second day on Outermost Isle, she was warm. Then she realized that she was again in the little coral house.

"Most strange," she thought, for she distinctly remembered falling asleep outside.

As she stretched herself more fully awake, her feet touched some stiff cloth. She sat up quickly and peered in the dimness. There, lying on the floor near her, were a long skirt woven from seaweed and rushes and her own little jacket.

She put them on. The skirt came down to her ankles and was surprisingly soft. But the jacket felt strange and stiff, for it had been too long under the sea. When she tried to button it, she discovered that the silver buttons had been replaced by shells.

Sianna gasped and put her hands to her mouth. There was no longer any question about it. She was being cared for by Dread Mary herself.

Somehow, knowing that made everything reasonable. And so Sianna determined to stay awake that night in order to meet the seawitch.

"First I shall thank her," she decided, "and then I shall

demand my mother's buttons back. For surely, since she has so many, three less will not matter."

Sianna spent the day tidying her home and collecting shells for decorations. She smoothed a path to the sea and lined it with hundreds of scallops, for they lay about the beach in profusion. She found half an old barrel washed up on the far side of the island, and thought she could use it for a chair, but it needed a cushion. So she puzzled out the weaving in her skirt and spent the rest of the daylight gathering sturdy seaweeds to use as threads. She stretched the weed threads between the legs of the table, knotted the threads to the legs, and thus laid out her warp. By then it was sundown and she could see no more to weave.

She stretched and made a great pretense at yawning, for she was certain Dread Mary watched from somewhere in the sea. In a loud voice she announced—rather louder than she had intended—"I think I shall go inside to sleep."

Laying the remaining weaving beside the empty plate and cup, Sianna walked slowly into the house. But once inside, she stealthily parted the curtain at the window and peered out into the night.

A full moon was rising, and the strand sparkled with a thousand little lights. These were shells reflecting back the moon's rays. And though it was night, the shingle was as bright as morn.

A strange hush settled over the isle. All at once even the constant drumming of the waves on the shore seemed stilled. Sianna felt sleepy. She reached into her jacket pocket and drew out two sharp shells she had hidden there. These she placed on the floor and then stood upon them with her bare feet. The shells pricked her soles, and the pain would keep her awake.

It was near midnight when a splash near the shore startled her. Something—someone—was approaching.

In the moonlight everything appeared larger than in the

day. It seemed to Sianna that a great monstrous fish was rising up out of the water. Yet it was no fish, she saw at last, but a mer-creature, part woman and part fish. The creature heaved itself onto the shore with its hands and wriggled farther up the beach.

While Sianna watched from behind the seaweed curtains of the coral house, the mermaid's tail sloughed off and two perfect legs appeared in its place. Then the seawitch, for it was indeed she, flexed and wriggled her feet slowly as if it hurt to move them. She bent her knees and moved cautiously at first. Then she came toward the hut.

In the moonlight she gleamed white as the belly of a fish. Her hair covered her back and breasts as she moved. And the only things she wore were strands of anemones she had braided through her long black hair.

7. Sianna's Trade

Dread Mary did not look so dreadful then, for her face was quite lovely and soft in the moonlight. She moved with the grace of a creature still in the sea, her motions slow and majestic. She seemed to float in the air as she would in a wave.

The moment she saw the seawitch, Sianna knew what she would have to do. All thoughts of thanking her fled. The girl crawled out the window, though the shells scraped her legs. She ran down to the sea where the mermaid had shed her tail.

Grabbing up the slippery, wet tail in her hands, Sianna called out to the startled witch in a voice that quivered with fear, "Dread Mary, I conjure you, take care. You shall not return to the sea till I have what is rightfully mine."

At the sound of the girl's voice, Dread Mary turned. She came slowly over to where Sianna stood and held out her hand to the girl. In the moon's light Sianna could see the delicate pulsing membranes stretched taut between each finger and on the witch's neck, close up under each ear, were faint red gill lines that beat in her heart's rhythm.

"Give me my tail, child, and I will not harm you," came

Dread Mary's voice. It was liquid and low and full of the sounds of the sea.

"You shall not harm me anyhow, mother from the sea." Sianna's words were braver than her voice. "I am not afraid."

"Take care, child, for there is much to fear."

"Give me my buttons and you shall have your tail."

The seawitch kept her hand stretched toward the girl, but a smile formed on her face. It was perhaps the first time in almost three hundred years that she had smiled that kind of smile. It was a fond smile, a smile of liking, a smile of respect.

"I will make you such a trade," said the witch. "Give me my tail."

"First swear," said Sianna, who could not read that smile in the moonlight and feared a trick. "Swear by all you hold sacred and true."

"I swear by the constant sea," said Dread Mary. "I swear by the tides that turn again each day. By the infinite grains of salt in the ocean and the multitude of grains of sand on the strand. I swear by the scales on each fish in the water and by the seaweed rosaries that sway in the sea. By all these I swear that I shall return to you what is yours if you but give me back my tail."

Sianna smiled then. "It is yours. I cannot hold it." And she gave the fishtail to the witch.

Dread Mary moved closer then and took the tail from Sianna. Their hands touched briefly, the girl's warm and soft, the mermaid's cold and rough. Sianna looked deeply into the mermaid's black eyes. They were fathomless, they were ageless. The mermaid smiled again as she slipped into the tail. Then she dove back into the sea.

8. A Strange Pact

In the morning when Sianna woke, though it was nearer noon according to the sun, she ate and drank what Mary had left. It was then she found the three small buttons at the bottom of her cup.

"Thank you," she called out to the sea. "Thank you for everything."

There was no sign that she had been heard, so Sianna rose and went down to the water's edge. She slipped out of her skirt and jacket and left them lying neatly folded on the shore. Then she waded into the water and swam with strong strokes out to the middle of the cove. The *Gardlann*, the golden king-lark, circled her head as she swam. Playfully she splashed water up at it, and it turned indignantly and flew back to shore.

Sianna took a deep breath and dived. As she went down, down, down to the bottom of the sea, she began to feel the wonder of it again. Little spotted fish and big bloated groupers swam by. A many-legged squid pulsed along near the bottom. And ahead Sianna saw the galleon which Dread Mary called home.

She circled around the galleon half looking for the bones

of the fishermen and half fearful lest she find them. But
bones and dead fishermen were as much part of the storyteller's art as was Mary's wickedness. At least that was how
it seemed under the sea to Sianna. She rose for a quick
breath, then dove again.

This time Sianna swam directly to the ship and, pulling
herself along the rail, came to the forecastle. Hoping that
at least that part of the legend was true, she knocked three
times upon the wood. But there was no answering knock.
The last bits of air in her chest were aching for release, and
so Sianna swam quickly to the top. Gasping for breath, she
was just deciding whether she was strong enough to go down
again when there was a loud splash behind her. Sianna
turned and there was the seawitch smiling at her and holding
out her webbed hands.

Without a word, Sianna took the hands in hers. Then
Dread Mary drew her down under the waves and together
they searched out the hidden caves and grottos of the deep,
played with schools of flying fish, rode on rays, and even
straddled porpoises for a race across the cove. Whenever
the girl tired, the mermaid would hold her up. Whenever
the girl grew short of breath, the mermaid would bring her
to the surface.

Later, when they were both exhausted from the swim,
they came ashore. The mermaid doffed her tail, and the two
played a game of tosses with an ivory shell.

While they were resting, Sianna made up a song for the
seawitch that went like this:

> *"My mother is the sea,*
> *And from her I have come.*
> *She feeds and comforts me.*
> *Her water is my home.*
> *She rocks me when I sleep,*
> *She holds me when I ail.*

She's big and wide and deep
And never shall she fail
        To comfort me, to come to me,
        Drifting down, derry derry down.

My mother is the sea,
And to her I shall go
When aught shall trouble me,
Seamother she will know.
She holds me when I drift,
And cushions every fall.
For giving is her gift,
Forgiving is her all.
        She comforts me, she comes to me,
        Drifting down, derry derry down."

When Sianna had finished, the mermaid clapped her hands with delight. "Another trade, dear child."

Sianna was silent for a moment. She feared the witch might want the buttons back.

But Mary, sensing her fear, said, "No, no. Here is my trade. You will teach me the songs of the shore, and I will teach you the spells of the sea. For ever, it seems to me, I have loved singing."

Sianna said, "But how long shall such an exchange take? I fear that my father's poor heart is breaking while he waits for me on the land."

The seawitch looked away. "Let the man be unhappy then. For it is not only women who are born to weep."

Sianna answered, "How can you say that? I do not want him to worry. Oh, seamother, he is but a poor button maker. But if you take me home, he will make you buttons enough to fill the entire sea."

Mary reached out for the girl's hand and held it to her breast. "Little songbird," she said, "do you know what it is like to be lonely? I do not think I knew until you came how empty my life has been. You are here and here you shall stay."

Sianna began to weep. Till that very moment she had thought of Mary as her friend. She saw now that she was not the witch's friend but her prisoner, for true friendship—like true love—does not seek to bind.

The mermaid was upset by the tears and wanted to stop them. She said slyly, "When you know as much about magic as I do, then perhaps you will be able to find your own way home."

"Do you believe so?" asked the girl, hope in her heart again.

"Oh, yes," replied Dread Mary, "though it may take a long long time." And only she knew that she lied.

"Then it is a pact," said Sianna. "And you will see, I will be a most apt pupil."

"Here is your first lesson. And it is the most important lesson of all," said the witch. *"Magic has consequences."*

"Consequences?" asked Sianna.

"Yes," said the mermaid. "All of nature is in a delicate balance, the good with the evil, the soft with the hard, the weak with the strong. If through magic you create an imbalance, nature itself will right the scales. So whatever you do—for good or evil—it will be counterpoised. If you forget all else, forget not this."

Sianna nodded.

The witch smiled. "Come then, little bird. Teach me that seamother song."

9. A Year of Spells

Thus a year moved slowly for Sian, far away on the Solatian shore. Never a word passed his lips, for never did a sign from Sianna come from the sea. And his eyes were as salty with tears as an ocean wave.

On the Outermost Isle, the year moved swiftly for the girl and the witch. They traded song for spell and spell for song. And no one could say which had the best of the bargain. For each bit of magic that Sianna learned, she gave a song of love or sorrow in return.

Sianna learned the language of seals and which weeds of the sea took away pain. She was taught how to make a poultice of sea mustard and how to draw out poison with a fishbone lance. She discovered that every living thing has two names, one it is called by the people and one it is called in a spell, and that the spell name is so powerful it could command even the sharp-toothed shark. The only thing she could not learn was to breathe under the sea.

But mostly Sianna learned that magic has consequences. That every strong action leads to a strong reaction, that every up has its down, that there is no evil that does not have a balancing good, nor a good that does not sow some evil in its turn. And finally, what Sianna learned about magic was that it was best not to use it at all.

True to her word, Sianna taught Dread Mary the old songs like "In the Meadow Green and Early" and "My Love Is an Apple of Sweet Delight." Sianna's young mind held the memory of every song she had ever heard. And though sometimes she added new words or whole verses to a tune, such was her kinship with each song that no one could tell where the old words left off and the new ones began.

The seawitch and the girl sang the Seven Psalms of Waking with great gusto each morn. All the bold gypsies' songs and devil-defeated songs were the mermaid's special delight. But the seawitch learned more than just the songs, though she could not have said what.

To learn all of Sianna's songs, the witch taught her more than she had meant. Usually they sat side by side at the water's edge, for it was easier for Dread Mary to stay in her fishtail. One day, as they sang by the water's edge, the witch said, in exchange for a particularly lovely tune called "A Morning in May," "I will tell you my button lore." It was all she had left to teach.

So she told Sianna of the Magic Three, the silver buttons that each gave a wish to the wearer. And she talked of other buttons known of old—the Button of the Great Magus, which granted the bearer the gift of invisibility; the Button of Delight, which, when consumed, lent reality to dreams; and the Button of the Sisters Drear, which, when dissolved in sweet wine, caused painful death.

"But are they just tales to frighten children?" asked Sianna, for she had learned from the witch that much of magic is merely that. "Or are they real? You yourself have told me that truth and tales are ofttimes mixed."

"Well, as to the others, I cannot say for sure," said the witch. "But I seem to recall that I once knew a prince who had the Magic Three."

"How could you forget something as important as that?" asked Sianna.

"Some things you forget because you cannot help it," said the witch. "And other things you forget because they cannot help you."

"I remember a song about the Magic Three," said Sianna, almost to herself. "But I am not sure I recall all the words."

"Sing it," commanded Dread Mary. Then in a softer tone she added, "For as you remember, I shall remember. One helps the other limp along."

So Sianna began the song of the Magic Three.

> *"Sad news there came to the king's own son,*
> *Sad news to his father's throne,*
> *For Madame the Queen had sickened and died*
> *And left them all alone.*

> *And did she leave them gifts of gold,*
> *All from her dowry,*
> *Nay she has left them naught for love*
> *Except the Magic Three.*

> *And One is for a mighty wish,*
> *And so be Two and Three,*
> *And she has left them to her son*
> *And dived below the sea.*

"But I never knew it meant buttons," said Sianna. "Isn't that strange."

As the witch sang the words back to her, Sianna put her hand in the pocket of her jacket and fondled the buttons she kept there. They were her only past, for with Dread Mary there was but the present day. And without thinking what she was doing, Sianna brought out one of the buttons and began to rub it with her finger. A bit of the black rubbed off. Below it the button gleamed dully.

As if in a dream, Sianna recalled her father saying, "Let me remember the cruel sea when I see them." She knew that she could answer him now, "The sea is not cruel." For cruelty and compassion were on either side of the scale and the one would balance the other.

So as the witch continued to sing back her song, and as she absently corrected the tune or the words, Sianna took up a handful of sand and water and scrubbed at the button some more.

Finally she polished it with the sleeve of her jacket till it gleamed. It had a design on it—a single fish. When she held it up to the sun, the silver button caught the light.

"What do you have there?" asked the witch, breaking the song in the middle.

"It is one of my buttons," said Sianna. "See, I have polished it. It has a fish on it. Isn't it pretty?"

The witch moved closer to the girl. "Give me," she cried, and snatched it out of Sianna's hand.

"But it is mine," said Sianna, her voice shocked and full of tears. "It was the first bargain we made."

"Little fool, it is one of the Three," said the witch. "I remember it all. It is mine." And with a mighty splash, she dove back into the sea.

10. The Wish

Sianna stood by the water's edge and called over and over for the witch to return. But she did not. And when the moon began to rise, Sianna walked slowly back to the coral house. She went inside and sat down to think.

She thought about all the witch had taught her, the spells and the simples, the language and lore of the sea. But mostly she thought about consequences. For she knew that, though the witch had one button, she still had two. But she did not know what she should do.

She did know, however, that she would have to guard the remaining two buttons from the witch. "They are my mother's, after all," she thought, for she needed a reason for her vigilance. "Isn't it strange that all this time I had the power to return home close to my hand." But she also knew that she did not yet *really* know how to use that power.

Then Sianna fell asleep and dreamed that the witch was standing by the door of the coral house gazing down at her with her lost memories found.

The witch remembered Melinna of beauty and song. She remembered Prince Anggard, who must surely now be king. (The one memory she did not have was of any time passing.) She remembered how well she had loved, how much she had given, and how much she had hated. Her bitterness welled up inside her like a salt spring.

"Magic has consequences," Dread Mary mumbled to herself. But, she wondered, what consequences should she fear? If all she planned took place on the far shore of Solatia, then how could it disturb what she loved on the isle? She wondered this but did not see that merely by snatching the button from Sianna she had already begun the wreckage of all she loved.

So she twisted the button in that certain way, left, then right, then right again. As she twisted it she said out loud, "Magic One of Magic Three, grant the boon I ask of thee." And the button twisted by itself under her fingers.

> *"Remove the king upon the throne,*
> *And turn his living heart to stone.*
> *Another king put in his place*
> *To be the last one of that race."*

As she said the words, Dread Mary smiled. She did not know that the king she cursed was not the king she remembered but a descendant of his cousin many times removed. But so great was her vengeful passion that she might not have cared had she been told. Dread Mary's face at that moment was indeed dreadful to see as she laughed with the knowledge of what was to come.

There was a loud clap of thunder round the isle, though the sky was clear of thunderheads. A clap of thunder as the button twisted in her hand once again. And then the button ran like quicksilver through her fingers and was gone.

Dread Mary smiled again in Sianna's dream and turned back toward the water.

But it was no dream. The thunder wakened Sianna fully, and she watched in the rising sun as the witch pulled on her fishtail and plunged into the sea.

11. The Great Wave

Down to the seashore Sianna raced, hoping to stop the witch.
She called to her but there was no answer. Then Sianna
heard a horrifying rush of noise as if the ocean were sending
its greatest monsters ashore. Bearing down on her was a
great wall of a wave. She had no time to call or scream
before it swept over Outermost Isle and carried her once
again into the sea.

This time she kept her skirt and jacket on, though the
fingers of foam tried to snatch them away. She fought against
the motion of the wave as it bore her from the isle.

Even as she fought, she was aware that the wave was
rolling on past the Triades, past the Mean Isles, past the
Inner Isles, toward the Solatian strand. She struggled to
reach into her pocket so that she might twist one of the
buttons and thus assure her safety. But the weight of the
water kept her arms at her sides, and so she rode at last like
a sea-wrapped cocoon on the crest of the mighty wave.

The witch had heard the boom of the wave as it heaved
itself up out of the deeps. She had smiled to herself as she
saw in her inner eye the wave sweeping over Solatia's shore.

For she knew this must be a tide called up by the magic to
remove the king from his throne.

But as the foot of the wave churned the deeps and sent
muddy reminders into her cove, Dread Mary, who had been
Melinna, remembered the rest. *The consequences*.

A sudden cold fear struck her. She rose to the surface
and looked around and saw the wave as it moved toward
the Solatian shore. Then, turning slowly, she looked behind
her to the isle.

The little coral house and Sianna were no more.

Melinna, who had been Dread Mary, swam quickly to
the beach. She heaved herself slowly onto the shore like an
aged and brittle thing. She sloughed off her tail and on two
weakened legs wandered about the isle. The strand was
scoured clean of life, many trees broken in two. The golden
lark circled disconsolately looking for its nest. Slowly the
seawitch returned to the seaside and knelt by her fishtail.
And for the first time in three hundred years, she began to
weep.

She did not weep salt tears as humans do, but tears of
purest water. And she wept until she had wept a crystal
pool. Then she dove into it without her tail and never came
up again.

The wave was hasting toward the Solatian shore, breaking fleets and fish with its foam. It flung itself onto the
castle on the cliff, covering king and courtiers and all.

And when the wave had retreated, it left many injured,
the king and all his cousins broken on the stone steps down
to the sea, and Sianna at her father's door.

"A life for a life," said Sian when he heard his daughter's
tale. Except for her name, which he had cried into her hair
over and over again, these were the first words he had
spoken in a year.

"But it was not the life she sought," said Sianna.

"Still, he was not a particularly good king," said her father with finality. "Perhaps his son Blaggard will be better."

"Perhaps," said Sianna, gazing out the window as she sewed the remaining two brightly polished silver buttons to the underside of her petticoat. "Certainly all our lives will be better."

"And how say you that?" asked Sian.

"It is the consequences of the magic," said Sianna. "Good balancing bad."

"I do not see how that will affect our lives," said Sian.

"But it has already, dearest Father," said Sianna with a fond smile. "The very first thing that Mary promised was that she would give me back what was mine. And you and Solatia are mine. I do not think she truly meant to keep that promise. But she loved me, and so this good balances her act of snatching away the button." She did not mention the power of the other two or that she knew how to use them.

"And I can help renew the lives of all who still live," she continued, "with the things that the witch taught me. The sea has many riches, and I can show all Solatians how to share them."

"And can you explain how the evil of the wave has been balanced in the kingdom?" asked Sian, though he thought he already knew.

"Because the wave has taken away the rusted relics of the war. Because the people can return to the land. And because there is but one heir to the throne, so there need be no more disputes over who shall be king."

"But how can the evil of killing the king and his courtiers be balanced?" asked Sian.

"Perhaps his son, Blaggard, will be a better king," said Sianna. "Or perhaps, if he is indeed the last of his race, what comes after will be better for us all. I do not know. For knowledge of what is yet to come is never granted to any man or woman alive. And the dead surely have no need of it. But this I was taught and this I believe—such evil will certainly be balanced."

"Well," said Sian with a strange catch in his voice, *"my* life will be the better for this magical balancing."

"How so, darling Father?" asked Sianna. She turned her face to him and smiled a sweet smile.

"Little songbird, it is simple. I have my daughter back. As if it had to be said. I have my daughter back as wise as she is beautiful, to lighten my days with her knowledge and her songs."

And Sianna's voice followed him out with a song as he went back to work in his shop.

Here ends Book I

BOOK II

The Hollow Man

Book II is for David

Contents: Book II

Before

In the kingdom of Solatia, where the sun rose first on the lowland farms, there ruled a young king. He was handsome but he was hard. His name in the old tongue was Blaggard, or *jest of the king,* for he had been born late in his parents' life. When his father heard of him, he had remarked to the queen, "Surely this is but a jest."

Those who loved him or feared him—which were one and the same to him—called him simply Gard. And they named him Gard the Guardian. And Gard the Great.

But his enemies, and they grew in number as his days upon the throne, called him Blackguard. And Bleakard. And the Bleak One. They talked this way only in whispers, for it was said that he had eyes at each farmyard and ears in each hall.

Both his enemies and his friends knew little of the king. His father had hated the sight of him, for he felt the boy's very existence mocked his old age. So the king had sent Blaggard away. The boy was banished to beyond the mountains, where he lived with wizards and warlocks. And as a young prince he had learned their ways.

But Blaggard was impatient, and so never learned the

most important lesson of all, that magic has consequences. And because he never learned it, he used wizardry where wisdom should have served. Until at last he had forgotten what wisdom he might have had. It was said, even by those who loved to praise the powerful, that Blaggard had been born under an evil star. However, he was not purposelessly evil. Rather, he coveted power, for as an apprentice magician and an exiled prince, he had lived long in power's shadow. So he played friend against friend and brother against brother to get power.

When Blaggard became king—by his own magic, so he liked to claim—he quickly put aside all whom he believed were more powerful than he. The wisest men he imprisoned. The wizards who had taught him he had cast from the castle cliff into the sea.

Blaggard had been eighteen years old when he ascended the throne, part boy and part man, "the worst parts of each," as the old Solatian saying goes. But now it was the seventh year of his reign, and it was seven years almost to the day when a great wave had carried away the old king of Solatia and broken his seven cousins upon the strand. A great week-long celebration was ordered for The Seven, as Blaggard named it. All the oracles agreed that it was, indeed, a magical time.

Even the Solatian farmers were eager to celebrate. It was not often that they would leave their crops thus. But the harvest had been full for the first time in seven years, and there would be more than enough for all the long Solatian winter. If the farmers did not like the king, celebrating his seventh year did not overly disturb them. They felt his hard hand when they paid their land tax and their crop levy, their seed tax and their gleaning. But for the most part they did not trouble themselves with affairs of the kingdom.

In the village, where Sianna and her father Sian the button maker lived, preparations for The Seven were already underway. By royal decree, ribbons hung from every door and bright banners flew from window poles.

Each house was decorated with the sign of a man's trade. The baker hung a basket of twisted buns on his front door for passersby. On long hooks outside the dyer's shop, skeins of colored yarns swung gaily in the breeze. The weaver had woven colorful headbands for the children and tacked them upon her door. And even Sian, who was usually too busy for celebrations and too cynical for ceremony, had placed upon the door jamb a pouch of free buttons made from the iridescent Solatian shells.

Sianna had been busy all day and half the night for a week before The Seven making simples and herbal teas for the villagers who had become sick from the excitement of the coming feast. Unlike her father, she enjoyed the company and was glad to help where she could.

"Bless you, Sianna," was the constant payment she received as she went from house to house with her remedies. Sianna would take naught for her healing except a song. And so it was she learned all the songs of the kingdom, which she wrote down in a great book. It was a task she had set for herself when she was thirteen years old.

"If we do not write them down, they will be lost," she explained to any who would listen. "And that would be the loss of our past. Of our fathers and our grandfathers and their fathers before them."

So the people blessed her wisdom and her generosity, her warmth and her love. They blessed her even as they feared her, too. For Sianna had spent a year with the witch of the Outermost Isle when she was twelve. And she had learned all the witch's secrets for a single song.

At least, that was what the people believed. And Sianna said naught about it to change their minds.

1. The King's Proposal

In the cheery kitchen of Sian's house was an enormous fireplace high as a man and as wide as the wall. Around its edges hung all the black pots and small cauldrons that Sian used to make their meals. For Sian was the cook of the house, though many of the neighbors laughed and called it "woman's work." Still Sian would say, "Food is for my pleasure as well as my belly. And it is no pleasure to eat what my daughter cooks."

But it was the only complaint he had of her.

Often when Sian got down the pots and pans and began to cook them a meal, Sianna would join him at the hearth. Then in her light, clear voice, she would accompany his stirrings with a song.

They were a happy pair. And though many a village woman had set her cap for the cynical widower, he pretended not to notice. And if Sianna had taken note, she never said a word.

But Sianna was already twenty years old, and it was long past time for her to be wed. Yet such was the fear of the Solatians that she was more witch than woman, only one lad had dared ask for her hand. He was a fisherlad named

Flan, with more heart than head.

"It is no matter," she said to Sian one day when they talked of it. "For there is not a lad in Solatia who makes me turn my head. Not even Flan. For though he is a good lad, he will never be older than a boy."

"Still," her father said, "I would love a grandchild to carry on my blood. You know I am a proud man. Proud of my line."

Sianna laughed then and Sian joined her. They both knew that his pride was not in the greatness of his line. They were farmers all. But there was pride in the fact that Sian and his father and his father's father before him were known for their true tongues. "Their aye is aye, their nay nay," the villagers said of the family. And it had always been so.

"A grandchild you shall have, that I promise you. But who the father and when the wedding, that I cannot say," said Sianna. She kissed her father's cheek fondly and went out to gather the herbs of the sea.

It was while Sianna was out harvesting her ocean crop that a messenger arrived from Blaggard the king. He was dressed all in reds and golds with a feathery hat and buckled boots. Never had Sian seen such a sight in his own home, for he was a poor man withal, and a messenger direct from the king is rarely sent to the poor.

The messenger did not so much knock at the door as plunge in. If he was taken aback by the sight of the tall, white-haired man dressed in a leather cooking apron, stirring the soup, it did not show on his face. For a man who serves such a king as Blaggard learns quickly not to show what he feels.

"Are you Sian the button maker, father to the maiden known as Sianna of the Song? The maiden who spent a year with the witch of the sea?"

Sian merely grunted.

"Then," said the messenger, making as much ceremony

as he could out of a simple task, "I am ordered to deliver this letter unto your hands in the name of King Blaggard."

"Well, man," said Sian "give it here." He had no patience with ceremony or wasted words.

The messenger handed the letter to Sian, who looked quickly at the red-and-gold seal. Then, sticking a cooking knife into the envelope, Sian slit it open.

The message said:

> I shall marry your daughter Sianna
> at The Seven. You shall attend me on
> the morrow to be instructed in the
> wedding plans. Your promptness shall be
> rewarded by a dukedom. Your tardiness
> by the dungeons. The choice is yours.
>
> HRH Blaggard

Sian continued to stare at the message long after he had read its contents. His daughter? His Sianna? He looked at the message again. Then he turned to the messenger, saying with bitter sarcasm, "And does he wait to hear my choice?"

But the messenger was no longer there.

2. Sianna's Plan

When Sianna returned at sundown from gathering herbs, she found the soup cold. Her father sat in the chimney corner, his head in his hands. His face in the shadows seemed long, and hollows were in his cheeks.

"Father, what has happened? What is the matter?" cried Sianna the moment she saw him.

Silently he handed her the letter. She could scarcely make it out in the gloom. Sian attempted stoking the fire, and warmth and light began to enter the dark kitchen.

"It is a great honor to wed a king," said Sian slowly.

Sianna looked at her father. "You know full well it is no honor to wed this king, this blackguard. He is a hard man with more power than wisdom. He has rid himself of all who might challenge him. I see he would silence me, too, though I am far from the counsels of the rich."

"I do not understand," Sian said. "What do you mean, *silence you?* And why should he want to marry you? There are many marriageable maidens among the families of wealth."

"I think he has heard tales of me in his great hall, as you have heard tales of him in our poor village. There are no

57

wise men left and there are no wizards left but Blaggard
and me. I fear he fears my powers."

"Is there aught in your powers to fear?" asked Sian.
"Herbs and simples . . . what have you ever done with them
that could cause fear?"

Sianna looked down at her strong hands and flexed her fingers. She thought of the two magic buttons she had sewn to
her linen petticoats, magic buttons that granted the wearer a
single wish—but with consequences. She had never told her
father of their power, though she had known of it for seven
years. It was the one secret she had kept from him.

"With magic, it is not always what you do, but what you
can do that makes men fear," she replied.

"Could you not change this king?" asked Sian. "Wed
him and change him?"

"I dare not wed him, Father. By wedding me, he would
also wed my powers to his. His years of learning were longer
than mine. His teachers many, mine but one. And so his
powers are necessarily greater than mine. As his wife, I
could only be changed, not change. That is the way of
magic, the greater eats up the lesser, drains it when touching
day to day. Whatever else takes place, *I must not wed
Blaggard*. It is not only for myself that I say this. It is for
all of Solatia."

"What is there to do?" asked Sian. "For I would gladly
go to the dungeon for you—if not for Solatia."

"Going to the dungeon, my Father, would not help. The
king would merely take what he wanted without your bless-
ing. No, I have a plan. But it will take much talking between
us this night if it is to succeed."

Sian nodded.

"For, you see, dearest Father, you must do something
that is difficult to do. You must tell a lie. And because your
name is well known for truth, you will be believed in this
lie."

Sian looked at the ground. He was not happy. He could not pretend that he was. But for his daughter, he would tell a single lie.

Early in the morning, Sian dressed carefully. He put on a clean linen shirt, freshly cleaned trews, and a leather jerkin held fast with leather buttons. He packed himself a half-loaf of brown bread, some goat cheese, and a flask of berry wine for his trip to the castle. Not that it was so far, but they neither of them knew when he would be home again.

They kissed swiftly and parted. Sianna could not walk with Sian to the castle because a woman in the village was about to bear a child, and as it looked to be a hard labor, the midwife had asked her to attend.

Thankful that Sianna did not watch him go, Sian went along the strand. At the foot of the one hundred stone steps that were carved in the cliff's edge from the beach to the castle, he stopped. Hand on his heart, he lifted his face to the sky and prayed. It was the first time in many years he had addressed himself to his god.

"I pray you guard my tongue as I would guard my daughter's life."

Then he went slowly up the stairs.

At last he reached the castle door. Seeing his letter from the king, the soldiers passed him in without a word. Silently he went through the many doors until he paused at the one to the throne room. Through the open door came the high sinuous piping of a flute. The melody was strange, compelling, and dark. Suddenly the flute broke off in the middle of a phrase.

"Don't stand there like a gawking bear," came a voice that for all its youth was unpleasant and oily. "I trust that your tatters and tears signify that you are Sian, my father-in-law to be."

And Sian walked in the door.

3. The Four Questions

"Why, he is but a boy," thought Sian, and his fears began to fade. Sianna must be wrong. For Blaggard was barely five-and-twenty years old. His face was beardless and comely; his gold hair hung down to his shoulders in well-brushed ringlets. In his right hand he held a flute carved from bone. He looked to be the perfect prince, and Sian was soothed by those looks.

There was a carefulness about Blaggard's entire person: the silken clothes just so, the legs crossed precisely in the middle. Almost as though he was afraid to be less than perfect.

"I assume," said Blaggard again, leaning carefully forward on his throne, "that your answer to my marriage proposal is *yes*, Duke."

"My answer," said Sian, remembering his rehearsal with Sianna through the long night, "is a question. Four questions, to be sure."

"Four questions? What do you mean?" Blaggard made a swift motion with the flute to the guards at the door. They entered and stood silently at Sian's side.

Sian was frightened, but not by the guards. He was afraid

his voice would betray the lie, for he had never told one before.

"My daughter follows the Old Way," he said. "And in the Old Way, the Elemental Questions must be answered satisfactorily or the wedding will never take place. Fire and flood and disasters more terrible than these have attended weddings where the Four Questions were not properly asked and not properly answered."

"What nonsense is this?" Blaggard said angrily. He turned to the counselor on his right, while his hand fidgeted a silent tune on the bone flute.

"It is true, your Majesty," replied the man hesitantly. "Some of the villagers used to practice what is known as the Old Way. Perhaps, since you were brought up beyond the mountains, you never heard of it. There are tales of great waves and shaking earth swallowing up false brides and bridegrooms, those who did not ask or could not answer the Four Questions. But such tales, perhaps, are not altogether true. The Elemental Questions, though, are purely ritual riddles, riddles about the four elements that make up the world—earth, air, fire, water."

"And what are the riddles and their answers?" asked the king.

"That I do not know, sire. They were part of the secret ceremony known only to the followers of the Old Way. I never followed it. Indeed, the Old Way was stamped out by your gracious grandsire years ago." The counselor bowed as if to signify the end to his knowledge.

Blaggard turned to the button maker. "Tell me the riddles, man."

Sian stared into the king's eyes, for only thus, Sianna had cautioned him, would he be believed in his lies. "That I do not know, your Majesty. I am not a follower of the Old Way. Only my daughter in all of Solatia holds to it.

She learned it from the seawitch, Dread Mary, when she was but a child."

"And four Elemental Questions must be asked and answered, old man?" said the king.

Sian nodded.

The king thought a minute. Then he laughed out loud. "Yes, there shall be questions, old man. But you did not say who shall ask them. And *I* shall ask them. Yes, I shall ask the questions. Of anyone else who would try to marry your daughter. She shall have till the last day of The Seven to find someone who can answer *my* four questions. At the castle fair she may invite as many as she dares. If there is anyone who can answer *my* questions, he shall marry your daughter and live in fine style with her here at my own castle. But I do not think there will be any who will be able to guess my riddles. And those who try and fail—shall die."

Sian gasped. Things had not happened as he and his daughter had planned, and he did not know what to say to make things right.

But the king dismissed him then. As Sian was led to the castle door, he heard Blaggard saying, "Come, my ministers. With your wisdom and my wizardry we shall make four Elemental Questions that even Sianna of the Song cannot answer."

4. The Castle Fair

For all the Solatians, The Seven had been a success except for Sian and his daughter. The merrymaking had been added to by the free casks of apple wine sent down from the castle. And not one of Sian's neighbors had thought to ask why the button maker's cottage was dark and Sianna and her father did not take part in the holiday. But, as Sianna herself had remarked to her father, "It is difficult to see another's pain when one is brimmed up like a wineskin."

But on the seventh day, Sianna and her father were summoned to the castle for the fair, and they could not refuse. Indeed, Blaggard sent guards to escort them, carrying pikestaffs twined with garlands.

Slowly Sianna and her father, flanked by the guards, made their way up the hundred steps. Neighbors and friends greeted them lustily. They were offered leather bottles half full of wine and joints of meat still warm from the spit. But Sian, dressed in a clean linen shirt, and his daughter, in a long white linen dress with yellow lace and crowned with seaflowers, looked neither left nor right. They marched stonefaced to the castle door, where they were greeted by the king himself.

"Come, my lovely," Blaggard said to Sianna and took her hand. "I shall have you dressed in silk like a queen. For queen you shall surely be before The Seven's last eve is out."

Sianna raised her head and stared into Blaggard's eyes. "I shall be wed in this dress and no other. I made it with my own hands after my mother's design. I wove the cloth and tatted the lace. The buttons are my father's work. What I came in, I shall go in. It is the Old Way. It is my way."

Sian was astounded. He had never heard such firmness, such power in her voice. At last he understood why Blaggard might fear her, and he wondered if Blaggard might not be right to fear.

Blaggard looked away from Sianna's strong gaze. "As you wish," he said, and forced himself to shrug.

The king led the two to a platform that had been constructed on the castle grounds. It had three steps. Blaggard sat on a throne on the topmost part. Sian and Sianna sat in carved chairs on the next. And guards and counselors stood on the bottom part of the platform.

A blare of trumpets greeted their arrival. The merry-makers at the fair bowed, and a group of dancers began to leap and twist, the bells at their ankles and knees making a merry company to their steps.

At the moment of the trumpets' sound, posters were hammered onto doors and pasted onto walls around the kingdom so that all at the fair and in the countryside could read at once:

BE IT KNOWN
that Blaggard the King
will wed the maiden known as Sianna
unless
there is a man who can answer the
FOUR ELEMENTAL QUESTIONS

before fall of night at The Seven.
To try and fail in answering the riddles will mean
Death by the Sword.

"You certainly do not encourage any who would try,"
said Sianna when she read a poster the king thrust into her
hands.

"I do not want such a prize as Sianna of the Song to
escape me," said Blaggard.

"And what makes me such a prize, sir?" she asked.

"Your beauty, your voice, your wit," he replied. His
mouth spoke the words, but his eyes were cold and gave
the lie to his mouth.

"My power," said Sianna quietly. But though she spoke
as softly as a creature of the sea, Blaggard heard.

"You have no power," he replied. He looked down at
the bone flute he wore at his belt. His hands touched it
lightly. "In this kingdom, only the king has power."

"Then why do you fear me?" asked Sianna.

"The king fears no one. Perhaps I *love* you," he said.
But there was loathing in his voice.

"It is a strange love that seeks to destroy."

Hate flashed brightly between them, and their words were
a deadly game they played.

Bartering and bear baiting, horse racing and wrestling,
juggling and jongleuring, and singing of songs went on all
day at the fair, but no man came forward to try for Sianna's
hand.

From all parts of the castle came the sound of laughter.
Sianna could not remember having heard so light a sound
in Solatia before, and each laugh seemed a knife in her
heart.

The sun was near setting, and the smile on Blaggard's
face grew broader and crueler. "Look, lady," he said to
Sianna, "how the sun sits heavily on the horizon."

"Not as heavy as my heart in my breast," she replied. Then she gave a start as a familiar figure moved toward them. It was Flan, the simple fisherlad who had long loved her.

"Oh, no, dear Flan," she said to herself, as a single tear filled her eye and moved down her cheek. "It is useless for you to try."

5. The Magic Two

Flan marched up to the throne escorted by guards. He smiled brightly at Sianna to calm her, but the sweet innocent look on his face served only to encourage her fear.

"I shall answer the Four Elemental Questions," he said. Then he quickly added "Your Majesty" when he saw a frown begin to form on the king's mouth.

"Fool," said Blaggard.

"No fool, but a fisherman," said Flan. He turned his smile on the king, for he had not the wit to fear.

"It is said that there is no fool like a fisherman," replied the king. "And I suppose it shall be proved out. Very well, here is the first riddle. Your head sits so lightly upon your body already, you will not feel its separation keenly."

"Do not worry, your Majesty, I shall not fail," said Flan brightly. "I already know the answers. My father found them for me in a book of great-grandfather's. Though all the other books of the Old Way were burned, my family kept this one out of respect for the old man."

"So you know the answers," said Blaggard slyly, playing with Flan as though he were a fish on a line. "But what if my questions are not your questions?"

"But that is not the Old Way..." began Flan.

"Silence!" thundered Blaggard, suddenly bored with the game. "It is my way." He turned and nodded at Sianna, then motioned the guards closer to Flan's sides. For the first time the fisherlad felt fear.

Blaggard leaned over and looked into Flan's eyes. With a careful gesture, he moved a misplaced curl to one side. "Here is a riddle for a fisherman," he said with disdain. "Answer if you can:

> *"A water there is which you must pass,*
> *A broader river there never was,*
> *Yet of all rivers that you might see,*
> *To pass it o'er is least jeopardy."*

Flan stared back at the king. Sweat beaded his brow. Finally he whispered in a hoarse voice, "My great-grandfather's book said the answer to the Elemental Water Question was 'the sea,' but I think that is not the answer to yours."

"You are right," said Blaggard.

Flan said with surprise, "I am?"

"You are right," repeated the king. "You are right that it is not the correct answer."

"Let me guess anew," begged Flan.

But the king dismissed him by raising the bone flute. "Kill him," he said.

"Wait," said Sianna. "Please." She laid her hand on the king's arm.

He drew away quickly. "Do you wish me to spare him?" he asked.

"Yes," Sianna said in a whisper.

"For my *queen* I would."

Sianna drew her hand away and clasped her skirt. She

knew the danger began here. If she were made to beg, made to give in, marry the king by her own wishes, her power would start to slip away. She looked down.

"Sianna, do not wed this monster," called Flan as they dragged him away. They took him to the top of the sloping hillock that led from the castle to the sea. Castle Hyl it was called.

The fisherlad's sudden courage spurred Sianna to action. "I will not," she whispered. "I dare not." She reached down to the bottom of her skirt and, slowly and carefully, pulled off one of the buttons she had sewn to her petticoat. She had hoped not to use it, to try every other path. But every other path seemed to lead to the king. Sianna straightened up.

"What are you doing, lady?" asked the king, suddenly suspicious.

"Wiping the hand that touched you," she lied.

The king turned from her and signaled for the swordsman.

At that moment, Sianna held the button between her palms. She thought briefly of the consequences her act of magic must surely call forth. But the consequences, whatever they were, seemed so far away and the need so immediate, she thought of it no more. Under her breath she said the words she had heard as a child, the magic words spoken by the witch of the sea. She looked as though she were praying. And as she spoke, Sianna twisted the button in her hand, left, then right, then right again. "Magic Two of Magic Three, grant the boon I ask of thee." And the button twisted by itself under her fingers.

> "Spare the lad whose name is Flan,
> Replace him with another man,
> One whose strength lies in his wits
> And can these riddles all untwist."

There was a sudden clap of thunder, though the sky was clear of storms. Then the button ran like quicksilver through her fingers and was gone.

It had all taken but a heart's beat to happen. The headsman was drawing his sword, the bright metal flashing in the rays of the setting sun.

But in its silver blade a sudden black reflection formed. A knight all in black armor on a horse so dark it seemed a shadow rode up the slope of Castle Hyl.

"Hold," he called. And so powerful and deep was his voice that the headsman held his sword.

6. The Questions Asked

"Hold yourself," roared Blaggard, jumping to his feet. "In this land no one calls *hold* unless he be king. And I am all the king here."

"I did mistake you, sire," said the black knight when he had ridden up to the raised platform. But he did not bow or even nod his head. Nor did he lift the visor that hid his face. He acted as though he were a king himself. His voice seemed to come from deep down within the midnight armor and echo there. "I did mistake you, for I have never known a king to so forget his own royalty as to behead a simple man for the crime of love."

Blaggard sat down carefully. "He is freed," he said, and waved the headsman away with his hand. "It was but a *blague,* a jest."

"You shall not jest so with me, sir. Say on your riddles, for I have their names in my head."

"Then you shall keep your head—and keep the lady, too," said the king. "But I do not think you shall long have either."

"Say on," rumbled the black knight. He was as impatient as Sian with wasted words.

"Your mouth is mighty anxious to part company with

71

your body," said Blaggard. He was relaxed again and smiling.

"I am mightily anxious to part company with you, sir king."

"By my flute, I should have you beheaded for your tongue," said the king. "But I think one parting from it will be enough. Answer this, then, if you can:

> *"A water there is which you must pass,*
> *A broader river there never was,*
> *Yet of all rivers that you might see,*
> *To pass it o'er is least jeopardy."*

"Dew," said the knight. His voice was low but could be heard all over the castle court.

Blaggard nodded unsmilingly. "That was the simplest. Even a fool could answer it."

Flan, who had hastened back to the throne, muttered, "Alas, I could not." He was signaled to silence by Sian, who raised a finger to his lips.

Flan was soon jostled by his friends and neighbors in the courtyard. And the merrymakers, who had been quiet since the headsman had first raised his sword, began to whisper together. They looked up at the black knight. The younger women glanced at him appraisingly. The men nodded with admiration at his horse and how well he sat the steed.

"Quiet!" roared Blaggard. "Anyone who speaks shall be thrust off the cliff. For this knight has guessed but one of four. He shall not be helped with the other three."

"I need no help, king. Say on."

Blaggard held out his hand. His chief minister hesitated, then climbed the platform and thrust a small piece of paper in the king's palm. The king glanced but briefly at it as if to prompt himself, then leaned forward. "The second question is," he said,

> *"What flies ever,*
> *Rests never,*
> *Sings as it goes,*
> *Moans as it grows."*

The black knight was silent for but a moment. Then he laughed, his head moving its iron case a little. "A child's *blague*, Blaggard. What answer but the wind."

The crowd murmured its approval. Flan clapped his hands together, and Sianna, who had been sitting taut as a kite's string, began to smile. She liked this strange knight, his deep voice, his brave, bold manner.

The king stood up. The crowd fell silent. Even Flan, in the midst of clapping, dropped his hands to his sides. The knight did not move except to put his mailed hands on his leg. The wind caught the blue-black feather in his helm and it danced impudently as if to mock the king.

"The third question is not a *blague*. Those two were just to tease. This one will separate the men from the lads."

Sian spoke then for the first time. "Say on, sire. For I think this be a man."

Blaggard with an angry motion lifted his flute as if to strike the old man. But Sianna turned in her chair and glared at the king with such ferocity that his hand faltered and he remembered himself. He lowered the flute and pulled a smile across his features, and then began to recite:

> *"High as a tree,*
> *Weak as a feather,*
> *Yet all of my men*
> *Pulling together*
>
> > *cannot pull it down."*

A child cried out from the crowd, "I know that." But before his voice had time to reach the ears of all, his mother had clapped her trembling hand over his mouth, so hard that her fingermarks could be seen there for a day.

Sianna and Sian leaned forward. Sianna's golden hair fell loose from the seaflower crown, and she twisted a lock of it so violently in her hand that she snapped six strands at once.

The black knight looked around him, at the men and women and the children who waited for his answer. At Flan, his hands clenched at his sides. Sian, sitting stiffly forward in his chair. At Sianna, her hair in disarray on her shoulders. At Blaggard, standing with a small smile of triumph beginning to show on his face.

"Smoke!" said the black knight. "And one to finish."

A shout went up from the crowd then, a shout that died as it was born, killed by the look from Blaggard's eyes. His hands made a magic sign over the heads of the people with his bone flute, and all froze. Whether by magic or by fear, no one to this day could say.

"Those were three childish riddles made up by my ministers," Blaggard sneered. "Ministers who shall be beaten for their lack of wit. A whip does much to make a man smart." He laughed at his own joke, but no one laughed with him. "But this last riddle is mine own. Answer it if you can.

> "It ventures forth upon the earth,
> Upon four legs it comes from birth.
> At noon, on two it climbs upon
> Until its earth time is 'most gone.
> At evening walks about on three,
> The fiercest creature this must be.
>
> *Name it!"*

As the last syllable died, the crowd took life again. The people swayed and clasped their hands. They sighed and looked down to the ground. But no one said a word.

Sianna sat unmoving, the only one so statuelike. Sian put his face in his hands and silently wept. The look on Blaggard's face was fully triumphant.

"That is indeed a difficult query," said the black knight slowly, as if stalling for time.

"Speak now," said Blaggard, "or be silenced forever."

Sianna moved then, a small hesitant motion as if trying to catch the knight's attention. Her hands fluttered like leaves at her sides. Her pointing finger stretched toward her father, toward the king, toward the knight, toward Flan. But if the black knight noticed, he paid her no mind.

"It is a difficult query," he said again. "But, Blaggard, it is *not* wholly your own. I am a reader of ancient tomes. And I recall a similar riddle put forth by a great beast in a faraway land."

There was a sound like *"Oooooh"* in the crowd. Hope for the knight, for Sianna sprang up again.

"Speak now," boomed Blaggard. "Your time is up."

The black knight dismounted his horse. He stood by the beast's side and raised his hand. His finger pointed straight at Blaggard. "The answer is *man!*" he said.

"Man," echoed the crowd.

Blaggard fell heavily to his throne. His hands clutched the arms of the chair. "Show your face," he commanded. "That I may look on it and know my enemy."

"Show it yourself, O king," said the knight.

Blaggard rose again and stepped down the three levels of the platform. He walked through the crowd and stopped before the knight. As if in a tableau, Blaggard remained motionless in front of the knight for fully a minute. Then he reached forward and threw the visor back.

The armor was empty. Only blackness, deep and hollow, was within.

"Why, you are nothing but a hollow man," said Blaggard with a loud laugh. "Come, Sianna, and meet your hollow groom."

7. The Wedding

Sianna put her hand to her head and set the seaflower coronet firmly in place. She ran her fingers through her tangled hair. Then she stood up, came down the steps to the courtyard, and quickly crossed to the knight.

Blaggard pointed disdainfully to the hollow armor. But when Sianna looked into the helm, she saw a shining shadow there. She turned and smiled at Blaggard.

"I shall be honored to wed this noble knight."

The look that passed between Sianna and the king was long and hard. And Sianna knew that though she had won for an instant, the battle was not yet over.

Blaggard turned his back to Sianna and announced to the crowd, "This day, as I promised, shall end with a wedding. All are invited. You shall be happy for Sianna because I the king command it, though she weds a man of no substance." Then he stalked off toward the palace, his ministers in a flutter behind him. They knew that whenever he played with words his anger was raging within him and he was not to be gainsaid.

The black knight mounted his horse. Then he reached down and grasped Sianna's strong hand in his glove. He pulled her up behind him, and she slipped her hands about his waist. Though the armor was cold to the touch, she felt a strange warmth.

The knight made a small clicking sound, and the black horse began to move. They galloped once around the castle courtyard to the cheering of the crowd. Then the horse picked its way slowly down the gentle slope of Castle Hyl into the sea. It waded along the shore until it came to the village. Then it paced to Sianna's door.

"Why, how did you know that I live here?" Sianna whispered into the knight's helm.

"There are many things I know, dear lady," said the knight. "And not just answers to foolish riddles."

"Then you know that I must go in and make myself ready for our wedding," Sianna replied.

"If you do not wish that wedding to take place," he answered, "I shall take you away to my kingdom as a sister."

"I must wed you," she said, "for Solatia's sake."

"If that is the reason, it is no reason," he replied.

"And for my own sake as well," she said.

"Then I am content."

Sianna slipped from the black saddle and went into the cottage. The knight stayed outside in the gathering shadows, rubbing down his horse and bringing it water from the well. But not once did he remove his armor or his helm.

Inside, Sianna brushed her hair with long vigorous strokes. She took off her dress and petticoats and washed herself slowly, as in a ritual. Then she put the petticoats on again, checking the last silver button to see that it was still secure, as was her wont.

Suddenly she put her head in her hands and began to weep. She had spoken bravely to the black knight, but here, surrounded by her familiar things, she did not feel so brave. She felt unsure and alone and wished her father were there. But he was still at the castle.

She wondered if marrying a stranger was to be the consequences of her act of magic. If so, it was perhaps a small price to pay for saving Flan's poor head from the sword. Yet this knight in black armor seemed so strong, so good, so understanding, so wise. And it mattered not at all that he was a shadow, for she knew that the old meaning of the word meant "protection." They still said in Solatia that if a man were in the king's shadow, he was well cared for. And protection was what she most desired now. Too, she could not help feeling, under her fear, excited and even happy by the prospect of wedding such a man. For never in all of Solatia had a woman ever had such a groom. She wondered if a happy wedding could be considered "consequences."

"What nonsense, Sianna," she scolded herself, and looked in the mirror that was set in a large iridescent shell. "You fear where there is nothing to fear. You have saved your powers. You are to wed a noble man. You have not capitulated to that wicked king. Smile then, and go out and greet your knight."

She quickly put her dress back on, pinched her cheeks to coax the color back into them, and braided purple and red anemones through her hair.

Then she walked outside where the first evening star shone down on her and her groom.

8. Blaggard's Men

Almost everyone in Solatia, neighbors and friends, fisher-folk and farmers, craftsmen and kingsmen, came to the wedding. They crowded into the king's chapel and joined in the wedding feast. But Blaggard did not come, neither to the wedding nor to the feast nor to the wedding dance that would last until the dawn.

Instead, he sent a minister to bid the guests depart early, against all Solatian custom. Then he called his counselors to him.

"This Sianna must be mine," he said, though he did not tell them why. For to tell them was to halve his power; to show them the extent of his need could rob him of his rule.

"She will not long be happy with a hollow man," said one minister.

"Remove his armor, which is all that holds him together," said another, "and he will be blown away by a passing breeze."

"Then he will drift off like smoke and leave her before morn," said the third.

Whether they believed what they said did not matter, for

they were used to telling Blaggard precisely what they felt he wanted to hear.

"My exact thoughts," said the king. "And since he must remove his armor to retire, we shall remove it for him for good while he sleeps."

And they all laughed.

So when all else in the kingdom was asleep, and even the village crier had gone to his rest, the king sent his three strongest guards to remove the armor from the chamber. This they did and reported that Sianna had slept soundly throughout.

"And was there a man by her side?" asked the king.

"My lord, there was nought but a hollow in the bed where her husband ought to have been," the one called Rolan replied.

Blaggard smiled slyly to himself.

But on the morrow, when Sianna moved about the castle with a bloom in her cheeks, talking and laughing with the shadows that danced around the sunlight, Blaggard was annoyed. By noon, as the girl spoke softly to sunbeams and conversed with empty corners, he was angry. And by evening, when Sianna looked to be as content as any new bride, Blaggard could scarce contain himself.

"Woman," he bellowed, "you talk to phantoms. You speak to shades. I hear nothing. Therefore there is nothing to hear."

"My lord," she said softly, and the very softness of her words was a threat. "You sought to remove my knight from my life as easily as you removed his armor, but it is not done so easily as that."

"I have removed him," said Blaggard. "There is nothing there. You mock me, woman. I shall not be mocked."

"Nay, my lord. I mock no one. You heard him before

because you *thought* he was a man. I hear him now because I *know* he is one."

Blaggard could give no answer. And so Sianna continued, "But give us leave to return to my father's house, and we will trouble you no more."

"Never!" said Blaggard. For he knew that even though he was not himself wed to Sianna, his magic could still overpower hers as their lives touched day by day. Besides, he had decided upon a new course of action, and he needed Sianna and her shadow man in the castle in order to carry it out.

"You shall remain here with your hollow groom," he said. "You shall remain until I command otherwise." He said it slowly and deliberately, his fingers playing silent tunes on the bone flute.

"It is you, my lord, who are hollow. For hatred and fear eat up the insides of a man and leave nought but a hollow shell."

"Out of my sight, woman!" he shouted. And so great was his wrath he might have struck her, but he feared the silence of the shadows beside her and the magic that she herself contained. So he turned quickly and strode away.

But that night, when all was quiet again in the castle, Blaggard called his three guards to him. "Tonight we shall see what it is Sianna sees," he said. "I had a potion placed in her dinner wine. She shall not wake until morn. Go you to their chamber, and where the hollow lies by her side, toss a bucket of colored water. When you see the outline of this man, strike for his heart. Strike quick, strike true, and you shall be well rewarded."

Then the king paid each man the gold coin which kept them in his service, and went to his own chamber to slumber deeply until dawn.

9. The Two Attempts

In the morning, the three guards returned to Blaggard. Their hair was disheveled and their clothing torn. There was fear in their eyes.

"Your Majesty, we did as we were told," reported Rolan. "Past the hour of one, we crept upon their chamber with a bucket of blood-red water. The woman slept as still as death. And by her side was a deep hollow as if some creature lay there. We tossed the water and a form did indeed take place. But it was no man, my lord."

"No man?" asked Blaggard.

The second guard, Andel, broke in. "It was a mer-creature, a giant fish, a veritable whale."

"A whale," said Blaggard. He began to smile. "A whale!"

"Yes, sire," said the third guard, Bran. "And it so pitched and tossed and leaped about, and blew hot air and cold breath upon us, that we were near to fainting. And when we tried to spear it as you commanded, it broke our swords in two with its terrible teeth."

"And like to break us, too," put in Rolan.

"We barely escaped to tell you," they all three said together.

"A whale!" said Blaggard, and he showed his teeth with such a laugh that the three guards stood amazed. Then they too saw the humor in it and, for the sake of the gold coins they hoped to collect, joined in the laughter.

Blaggard was suddenly calm, but the three guards were caught in their laughs and their mouths shut quickly and they hiccoughed.

"Tell my ministers," said Blaggard, "that they are to call Sianna a 'fishwife' today."

Quickly the word was spread. And when Sianna arose at last from her drugged sleep and moved about the castle, she heard ministers as well as scullery maids calling her a fishwife. But she held her head high and gave them each such a sweet smile in return that even the bravest amongst them stopped at once and smiled back.

When Blaggard heard this, he was angered anew. He called the three guards to him again and told them that they would have to creep into the chamber once more that very night.

"But the whale, sire," said Rolan.

Blaggard did not tell them that the whale was but the result of magic. That the water had called to kind, and so the knight had *seemed* a whale. For in magic, fully a half is seeming. He did not tell them, because he did not want to share his knowledge with them, for he believed that sharing diminished his power. But he swore to them that there would be no fish this time.

"*This* time," he said, striking his thigh with the bone flute, "you shall not throw water on the creature. This time carry with you a silken net."

The following morn, the guards returned to the king. Rolan had a great gash in his leg. Andel was holding his arm. Bran had a blackened eye.

"Your Majesty, once more we did as you commanded.

Past the hour of one we crept upon the two in their chamber with the net of silken weave. The woman slept in her death-like sleep, and by her side was the hollow. And though it fair made our blood run ice in our veins to look upon that cursed hollow, we flung the net onto the bed. A form did take place, my lord, but it was no man. And no whale, either."

"What, then?" asked Blaggard. "What form?"

Andel spoke in a harsh whisper. "It was a creature of the air, sire. A giant bird. A veritable gander."

Blaggard laughed out loud. "Ha, ha! A gander!"

"Yes, sire," said Bran. "And it rose up with its wings making broad strokes in the air. The great webs of its feet and the strong bill ripped the weave in a moment. It laid about with such great shrieks, I thought it would call in the whole castle. It fair broke Rolan's leg and Andel's arm. And near put out my eye."

"A gander," said Blaggard as if he had not heard the rest, or cared. He showed his teeth. The guards laughed with him then, in spite of their wounds, for when the king laughed it was always best to join in.

Again Blaggard quit at once and said, "Tell my ministers to spread the word. Sianna is but a 'goosegirl'!"

And so the word was spread by morn. As Sianna went about the castle and out of doors and down to the village to visit with her father, she was mocked by friends who, though they might fear her, feared the king's magic more.

"What does this mean, Father?" asked Sianna when she was alone with Sian.

Sian looked carefully about at the shadows as if to make sure the black knight did not lurk nearby. "Alas, they say you are married to no man at all but a giant bird. They say I will have no grandchildren but goslings that the king will cook and eat for dinner. They say . . ."

"Then they say foolishness," said Sianna. "Dear Father, do not fear. For my husband is a man, though I do not know his name or his land. And though he was but a shining shadow at first, each day that I love him he becomes clearer in my eyes. He is tall and bearded, and black are his eyes and hair. There is a strange reticence about him. He will not speak of himself and has cautioned me not to question him. But for all his secrets, he is a good man. And I love him dear."

"Then why do the people say all these things?" asked Sian.

"I do not know," she replied. "Except that it be magic. And magic is mostly seeming. Perhaps he *seems* a bird to those who do not know him. Or perhaps the king would have it *seem* that way."

"I do not understand this *seeming*," said Sian, taking her hands in his. "Except that you *seem* content, and that is all that matters to me." And he kissed her cheek.

Then he looked at his daughter sternly. "Still, if your man is as good as you say, he will tell you what all this *seeming* is about."

Sianna looked down. "I dare not ask him anything about it," she said. "It is the one condition he has laid upon me."

"But then what is to be done?"

"I do not know that," she replied. "But this I do know. For two nights I have lain as one dead and have not seen the stars. I fear that I have been made to sleep by a potion too powerful to resist. But tonight I shall wear this amulet upon my breast." She showed the small stone to her father. "I have blessed it with words the seawitch taught me. It shall keep me awake, though I seem to sleep."

"Then go with luck, my daughter," Sian said.

"I will go with whatever is given me," she replied.

10. The Power of the Flute

The night came swift and starless. The castle darkened and all within were held in the "little death," for so the Solatians called sleep. Only in the king's chamber were four men awake, Blaggard and the guards Bran, Andel, and Rolan.

The king played a languid piping on his flute, and the men listened as if caught in a spell.

Scarce the stroke of one had faded than the king nodded to the three. They got up from the seats where they had rested, reluctant and yet eager to be done with the night's business. Only Blaggard himself seemed at ease.

"I shall accompany you this time and see that it is done well."

Then, silent as shadows, they moved down the long, empty corridor to the wedding-chamber door.

The door creaked open, but the chamber was silent as a tomb. Sianna seemed as deep asleep as before, and only she knew that the amulet kept her awake.

The three guards crept to the great canopied bed in the center of the chamber. They stared down at the hollow that mocked their eyes. Blaggard entered behind them and stood by the side of the door, hidden by the shadows and wrapped in some strange dark magic.

"Now," whispered Rolan, and the other two flung a sack of dirt they had carried up from the ground below.

As the dirt splattered upon the bed, Sianna drew in a quick breath, but in the tumult that followed it was never heard. For as soon as the dirt struck the hollow in the bed, a dark and bearded man, beautiful and fierce of body, took form. For the dust had called to dust, and he became fully man.

In a single leap, the black knight, the man of earth, leapt from the bed and laid about himself with such ferocity that Bran was thrown to the floor and Andel fled to the door. Only Rolan was left to defend himself with arms thrown above his head. Yet strange to tell, once the men had fled, the knight did not follow. He did not seek to press his advantage, but merely stood his ground.

Seeing this, the three guards wondered if they should charge again. Just as they were readying themselves, the king stepped forward from the door.

"Hold," he called, and raised his flute to his lips. As if caught in a dream, all held still. The king began to blow into the flute. A song piped and snaked out of it, a band of dark music that twined round and round the room like a blind serpent seeking its prey. And then it found him, the black knight standing with his arms crossed before him on the marble floor. The dark ribbon of music wound round and round and bound him fast. And when he was fully bound, Blaggard took the flute from his lips and smiled. He walked over to the black knight and said, "Kneel."

"I kneel to no man with a heart like yours," said the knight. "I kneel only through love."

"Then die," said Blaggard, and raised his flute like a sword.

As he had taken the flute from his lips, Sianna was
released from the music's spell. She thought wildly that she
must pluck the third button from her petticoat and wish upon
it. But the petticoat was across the room and she could not
get to it in time. All that was left was to take the blow upon
her own head, and she scrambled from the bed. But she
was not fast enough. For even as her foot touched the floor,
Blaggard brought the bone flute down upon the knight's
head and it cut like a sword.

The castle rocked with an invisible blow. Sianna was
thrown back upon the bed, the three guards upon the floor.
And when the castle was quiet once more, the king was
gone. Disappeared. And no one had remarked his leaving.

Rolan and Andel and Bran were weeping near the door-
way, for reasons they could not quite say. Noises came from
the hall as the castle folk woke to seek the answer to the
shaking. Only Sianna was dry-eyed and still.

"Sianna, beloved," came a cracked voice from the floor
where no man could be seen.

She came off the bed and knelt by the side of a shimmer
that began to fill the room with its light.

"Do not be sad," said the voice. "I am returning to my
own kingdom where I rule over all who have lived and will
live again. It was but for the power of the button that I came
at all."

She looked down at the light that seemed at once so
familiar and yet so strange to her. In the back of her mind
she heard the three men weeping at their own loss. "Then
I shall use the Magic Three and keep you here for good,"
she said.

"Nay, for who knows what consequences that would yet
call forth," the voice replied. "Besides, it is time for me to
go."

"Then take me with you," Sianna replied.

"Nay, beloved, not yet. For you shall bear our son," said

the voice, becoming stronger as it faded. Or so it seemed to Sianna, though she could not think how this could be so.

"Our son," she said in wonder, and then in hope: "How I do wish it."

"And he shall be the one who shall avenge his father, though he must do it with no thought of vengeance but out of friendship and love," the light said.

"Can such a thing be so?" Sianna asked, trying to hold the light in her hands and yet finding nothing to hold on to.

"It must be so," the voice went on. "There is no other way, for vengeance destroys those who seek it. Do not teach our son of hatred and revenge. Teach him rather of friendship and love, and he will accomplish it all."

Sianna felt the light dying as it grew brighter still.

"Call him after the first living thing you see at his birth," said the voice.

Then with a giant bursting, like a dying sun, the light was gone. The dark was suddenly colder and deeper than any Sianna had ever known. Yet the memory of the light burned within her and kept her warm.

"Come," she said to the three men as she stood.

They knelt to her first, then rose.

"We did not know, My Lady," said Rolan haltingly. Andel and Bran were unable to speak at all.

"We know now," she replied quietly. And they went down the corridor to seek out Blaggard the king.

11. And After

But Blaggard was not to be found. Not in the castle or in the village or on the Solatian shore. For days the dogs bayed and howled down the paths of the forest and out toward the New Mountains. After several weeks, the Solatians accepted that he was gone, taking naught but his magic flute and the robes that he had worn that night.

"Did he fear your vengeance, My Lady?" asked Rolan. Since that night he had become Sianna's self-appointed protector.

"Revenge exacts a harsher price on those who seek it, Rolan," she replied. "For so my knight cautioned me. You heard the same as I."

"But surely you hate Blaggard and us who killed that king you wed."

"I sorrow. I do not hate," she said. "For have we not all lost him?"

And Rolan knew then that she spoke the truth and understood why he had stayed to protect her. At that moment of first seeing the black knight in his own true body he had known that there was a man beyond all others whom he could follow for no pay but the pride of doing it. And he swore then that he would find that king and his kingdom or die in the attempt. He had forced Andel and Bran to swear the same. They were gone the following year and never heard of again.

It was when the Solatians were certain that Blaggard was gone for good—whether from fear of his life or loss of his powers they did not know or care—that they came to the button maker's door.

"Sianna," they called. And the leaders cried out, "Madame." They would have made her queen.

"I shall not be your queen," she answered. "For alone I do not have the wit. But with the help of four others, chosen from amongst you freely, I shall rule with what wisdom I do have."

So three of the old wise men freed from the king's dungeon and an old fisherwoman named Vivianna ruled with her. They met every few days in the castle's throne room, seated about a round table so that not one nor the other was at the head. They did not count voices as had been the custom in Solatia whenever several folk got together to decide on a plan. Nor did one person instruct the others what to do. Rather, they would talk and argue and persuade until all agreed to a single way. And if it was slow, it was fair. It was soon known through all the neighboring kingdoms as "the Solatian way" and everybody praised it, though not many tried it themselves.

And when it came time for Sianna's child to be born, she would not stay inside upon a bed as most women in Solatia did.

"Let me lie on a bed of sweet moss by the sea," she said. "For the salt air is healthy for living things."

And reluctantly her father agreed.

"And let only the midwife and my father be by," she

warned her friends, for she thought in that way she might look at Sian when the child was born and so name it after her father.

So it was that on an early morning in spring, she lay in labor by the side of the sea, her child being born to the rhythm of the waves. Suddenly a golden bird flew to her hand from one of the offshore isles.

"It is the golden bird from Dread Mary's isle," said Sianna with wonder in her voice.

"It is the *Gard-lann,*" said the midwife and Sian at once.

And at that very moment the child was born.

So he was called Lann after the bird. He was big and dark-haired like his father. But his voice was as sweet and happy and pure as any bird that sang on the Solatian strand.

Here ends Book II

The Crystal Pool

Book III is for Adam

Contents: Book III

Before

All along the sea that marks the eastern border of Solatia there lies a strand. It is of sand and stone and the dust of iridescent shells. The Solatian children, tanned by the sea-shine of a hundred sunny days, play along the shore. Whether of fisherfolk or farmer stock, the children love the sea. It is only as they grow older that some learn to fear it.

The sea is the great mother of Solatia, and many of the sweetest songs are sung in her honor. Not a feast day goes by that she is not serenaded. Indeed, especially at the Thrittem, the ceremony of manhood which Solatian boys all celebrate, are the old sea songs sung.

Of all the boys who were to celebrate their Thrittem in the coming year, none had a voice for singing like Lann, the only son of Sianna. From his birth on a mossy bed by the side of the sea, young Lann had arisen singing, or so they said in Solatia.

He was a wonder, was Lann, with his dark eyes and black hair, so black the like had never been seen in Solatia. For though the fisherfolk were dark, they were fair compared to him. And none could sing so well.

His voice was so pure and clear that not a day passed

that a helpful neighbor did not press upon his mother that
he should be apprenticed to a minstrel. But she could not
bear the thought of parting with the lad, for since his birth,
her own father had wasted away till now he lay all day on
a slat bed or sat on a bench outside the house, which over-
looked the sea.

By chance one day a wandering minstrel had come to
Solatia seeking to sing for the king. But he was told that
the king was gone some seven years—disappeared in fire
and flame, said some. Others claimed he had drowned at
sea. No one knew for sure. So the minstrel turned to leave,
and walked down the iridescent strand. He saw the children
playing on the shore and heard the boy Lann singing as he
played. So beautiful was that untrained voice that the minstrel could not help himself, and followed the boy home.

The boy's voice drew him to a cottage in the village
where an almost equally pure voice called out in return.
The new voice, a woman's, seemed to entwine about the
boy's. The minstrel added his own sweet voice to the two.
And when they had finished the song, the three looked upon
one another: the woman with golden hair but slightly faded;
the boy, dark and quick like a bird; the man worn with
wandering, his face a patchwork of lines. They looked upon
one another, and smiled, and the minstrel stayed.

Chando was his name. And he lived from then on near
the cottage. Not quite father. Not quite husband. But more
than friend to them all.

1. The Old Spell

It was Lann's thirteenth birthday, the time of spring planting. The sun sat in the sky like a golden kite. Sianna and Chando carried her father, Sian, out into the day, for the warmth of such a sun was good for him. They set him on a painted bench in the front of the cottage, facing the sea.

"Rest, Father, and breathe in the spring air," said Sianna. "Presently we shall go to the chapel for Lann's Thrittem. He is there now, making ready."

"That I am still alive for this day is enough," said Sian. "I do not need to hear him sing his part."

"But he needs you to hear him," said Sianna.

"The boy draws his strength from you," said Chando. "Surely you know that."

"You speak better than you know," said Sian, and he sighed.

"What do you mean?" asked Sianna, for she had never heard her father talk this way before, and she was worried that he no longer had the will to live. She knew that, despite her knowledge of simples and herbs, it was only his strong will that was keeping him alive.

"Sianna, daughter, there is a secret I have kept from you

101

all these thirteen years. But now it is time for you to know."

"A secret, Father?" Sianna sat down before the old man and held his hands in hers. "If it is a secret, and you have kept it so long, then perhaps you should not speak it now."

"Ah, but I must, for I fear I am dying at last."

"You are not dying, dearest Father. But if it comforts you to speak, then say on. Chando and I will listen."

Sian sucked in a deep draught of the fresh spring air. It seemed to give him strength to go on. "The day the young magician-king Blaggard disappeared, it is well known that no one ever saw him again."

"That is true, Father," replied Sianna.

"That is not true," Sian said. "*I* saw Blaggard that day. For when he disappeared from the castle, he appeared at our door."

Sianna's face grew taut. Chando put his hand on her shoulder. "For what purpose, Father?" she asked.

With a sharp movement of his hand, Sian signaled her to be still. The effort seemed to tire him. He wanted to continue the story at his own pace. "He appeared at our door and he called to me. I did not know who it was so early in the morn. I rose to let him in. He stepped into the cottage and raised his cursed bone flute and hissed these words at me:

> "*'Your life for his life you shall give.*
> *One man alone in this house shall live.'*

"I did not know then what he meant. I feared later that my life had been traded for your wedded lord's. And indeed, when you came home with no husband and no corpse, I thought *that* the worst. So I told you naught, fearing you might hate me for it. But when Lann was born, I began to understand what that wizard had meant. For each day that Lann became nearer a man, I became less. And because

Lann was dear to you and dearer to me, I said naught, fearing you might hate the child for it."

"Father Sian," broke in Chando, "know you not your own daughter well enough to see there is no hatred in her?"

"Tush, man," said Sianna. "There is hatred in every man if you push deep enough. And love, too."

Sian continued as if he had not heard them. "Today is my grandson's birthday. This is the year he becomes a man. One year from today he will be confirmed in his manhood. And the wizard said, 'One man alone in this house shall live.' I feel an icy clamp upon my heart. I will not last out the year." He fell silent.

"But what more, Father, what more?" cried Sianna.

"Hush, do not trouble him further," said Chando, his own short anger gentled. "Is that not revelation enough?"

"No, dear friend," said Sianna. "In magic there is always a chance." She held her father's hands tightly and said, "Father, if Blaggard cursed you, he still had to leave you with words for the cure. Say on, Father. What words?"

The old man looked confused. He had come to the end of his recital and had exhausted himself. He had nothing more to say. "Words?"

"What more did the foul magician say?"

"Nonsense, Sianna. None that made sense, even now."

Sianna shook her father. "Tell me this nonsense. For what means naught to you may mean all to me."

"Something about

> *'A living death no comfort brings*
> *Till bathed in a crystal pool that from*
> *the salt sea springs'* "

"What does it mean?" asked Chando.

"I do not know," Sianna replied. "But this I do. None of my balms or simples or herbs will aid my father. Unless we can unriddle this riddle, my father will be dead before the year is out."

They were so deep in their talk that they had not noticed Lann's return from the chapel. And though he had not heard the first, how his every breath sucked life from his grandfather, he heard the second. And a thought was born in him that day, a pledge to be made at his Thrittem.

2. The Thrittem

"Grandfather, Mother, dear Chando," the boy called out as if he had just come upon the three. Sianna jumped up guiltily, and Chando rose to his feet with great reluctance. Only the old man seemed at ease, as if a burden he long carried had been removed from his back.

"What is it?" asked Sianna, much more sharply than she had intended. For it was usually her habit to speak softly with her boy and instruct him with love and not pain.

"Why, it is time for my Thrittem," Lann replied. "And as I must, I have come to lead my family to the chapel. You know, Mother, it is ever the way."

Sianna smiled then, for her sharpness had been only her fear that the boy might have overheard their talk. And surely he could not have heard, with such innocence shining in his face. She gave him her hands.

"Gladly," she said, and added, "my man." Then she withdrew her hands and made a seat of them with Chando. Lann helped Sian onto their arms, and they walked to the chapel door.

As they went inside, Sian looked around. "It has been many a year since I came to this place," he said. "It looks quite changed. I swore never to enter again when your dear mother was swept away by a wave. I see I am forsworn."

"I think all will be forgiven on a Thrittem day," said Sianna. "For is it not written that *Nothing is forbidden on Thrittem save a lie*."

Sian laughed. His hand trembled on Sianna's shoulder. "Put me down with care on one of those benches," he said, pointing to a back row that was partially filled with neighbors.

"Nay, Father," said Sianna. "You know I am an elder and sit on the facing pews. So come you and sit by me, for any wit I have to be called Elder, I have got from you. And perhaps you will feel called to speak now that you have returned to the chapel."

"I have returned but for a day," Sian reminded her. "I am too old and weak to change my ways. But, for you, I shall sit facing. However, I do not think I will say a word. This is Lann's Thrittem and I should hope all would be silent this day to hear *his* words and *his* songs and *his* Great Pledge. At least, that was how it was done in my day. Have they changed that, too?"

The three moved to a front row on the facing side, the side opposite the double doors of the chapel. They nodded to their friends and neighbors as they passed.

"Nay, Father Sian," whispered Chando, "it is the same. But upon occasion, some wise person does stand and offer the boy a word on his Manhood Year."

"Aha!" said Sian. "Listen to the songmaker. Six years he lives by us, and he thinks he is a Solatian." It was an old joke between them.

But before Chando could reply, a hush fell upon the gathered men and women and children, for Lann had come into the middle of the room. In the space there, around which the benches faced, he stood tall and unsmiling. For to smile during one's own Thrittem, though not forbidden, was never done.

Sianna sat next to her father, her hands clasped together. There was a serenity on her face that belied her racing heart.

And then Lann began the traditional songs. He sang "Come Make Me Man" and chanted the old tale of the first Thrittem, when the Solatian god had come down from the sun and had grown as a Solatian child. He had made a pledge as a boy to lead the people to a new land. That new land had been by the sea, where the Solatians, who had been starving, learned to fish and to farm the ocean crops as well as sowing upon the land. And this was why the sea was called by them Great Mother. Then the Solatian god-child had talked of returning to his home, and on the last day of his thirteenth year, he dived into the sea and was drawn back up into the sun, never to return. Finally Lann sang the song called "A Year of Growing," which was the prelude to the pledge.

When he had finished the chanting and the songs, and only the echo of his clear, sweet voice remained in the ears of the assembly, Lann smiled. Then he said, as all boys did on their Thrittem, "This is my pledge: a year of growing, a year of going, until it is fulfilled. Great Mother, grant that it be so."

Sianna sat up straighter. Chando reached across Sian to hold her hand. For no one ever knew what a boy might pledge on his Thrittem. Even the priest who helped him learn the songs was not told ahead of time. And sometimes the pledges were foolish, and sometimes they were strange, and sometimes they were filled with sweet reason, but always they were honored throughout the year and fulfilled.

"I pledge to search for the crystal pool that from the salt sea springs. For as my grandfather has been cursed, it is only thus that he shall be saved."

"No, Lann," shouted Sianna, and she leaped up. Everyone stared at her, for never had a boy on his Thrittem been challenged in his pledge.

Lann moved over to his mother and stood before her. There was love in his eyes as he said, "It is *my* Thrittem. It is *my* pledge."

She reached out to him and held his hands. "So be it, my child. You have your father's strength."

3. Lann Prepares

That afternoon, there was feasting and dancing by Lann's house, for so was the custom. But Sianna could not smile and laugh with their neighbors and friends. Yet she could not weep either, for her way was one of action, and what could not be changed must be aided. And as she was a wise woman, and a wizard as well, she sought to prepare a great gift for her son that he might be protected from the dangers of his quest.

While the others danced and played on reed pipes and sang the old Solatian songs and drank more of the apple wine than was good for their heads, Sianna stayed alone inside the cottage. She pulled out strands of her hair and braided a strong chain. When the chain was finished, she bent down and pulled up her petticoat. There, sewn on the underside, was a silver button. No one but Sianna knew of its existence. It was the most powerful magic she had.

She ripped it from her petticoat and threaded it onto the chain. Then she knotted the chain securely and said a quick spell that it might never break.

"Lann," she called out the window to her son. He came to the window. "Come inside and close the door behind you," she commanded.

He came around the side of the cottage and in through the door quickly, though he did not know why he had been summoned. He feared his mother would try to persuade him from his quest. "Mother, I *must* go," he began.

"Indeed you must if you believe you must," she said. "I will not hold you. For there comes a time when a boy and his mother must part, though neither may agree upon that time."

"Then why did you call me here?" he asked. "Away from our guests." The singing and dancing had quite taken his mind away from the fearsome task he had set himself. He was half angry with his mother for reminding him. But in the darkened cottage, his petulance did not show and he looked far older than he was.

He looks, thought Sianna, a lot like his father if he but had his father's beard. Then she shook off that thought, for useless pining was not her way, and she held out her hand.

"Come, my son, and take this quest gift from me. I have but a moment to tell you of its power. So listen with care. You know already the one most important lesson of magic— that *magic has consequences*. And powerful magic has more powerful consequences than you or I or any wizard could know."

The unhappiness and anger had faded from Lann's eyes. It was replaced with concentration. Except for his singing, there was nothing Lann liked more than talking with his mother about magic. "This you have often told me," he said, "when you have taught me of simples and spells."

"Then listen to this which I have never taught you," said Sianna. "Know you the old song *'The Magic Three'*?"

"Oh, yes, Mother," said Lann, and began to sing softly:

> *"And One is for a mighty wish,*
> *And so be Two and Three,*

And she has left them to her son
And dived below the sea..."

He broke off, saying, "It is an interesting tale."

"It is no tale," she said, "for this—" She held out the necklace with the button. "This is the Magic Three."

"But, Mother, how do you know?" asked Lann.

"Know that I know."

"And where are the Magic One and the Magic Two?" Lann asked again.

"Gone. Used up. And the consequences have been dear. I know it all too well."

"Then say on, Mother, and as always, I shall listen."

So Sianna sat with her son by the cooking fire and told him of the power of the button. She showed him how he should say the spell and twist the button in a certain way to make the magic happen. And with their heads in the light of the fire, it was hard to say which was the older, for they both looked old and young, old with knowledge and young with hope.

Then Lann arose, and Sianna with him. "Do not use it lightly, Son," she said again. "Its consequences may be too hard to bear."

Lann put the chain around his neck and tucked the button inside his shirt. "I shall use it only if there is no other way left. Be assured, I shall try every path before the path of the Magic Three."

"I am assured," she said. "And all my love go with you on this most precious quest." They walked out to greet their guests and soon entered into the singing of songs.

Only occasionally did their eyes meet, and the knowledge that flashed from the one to the other reassured them both.

4. The Shell Compass

Before morn, Lann was up and away. He had stopped only to place a light kiss on his mother's cheek and pass a hand over his grandfather's brow. Then, a small pack on his back, he walked down to the strand.

He was surprised to see Chando there, sitting on the beach, his lute by his side. He was trickling sand through his fingers.

"Welcome, my almost-son," said Chando. It was ever a greeting with them.

"You knew I would be off this very day?" asked Lann.

"With as strong-minded a mother as you have, it is best to be off before she makes you stay," said Chando. "Besides, I was off the same way many years back. Though not, I am afraid, for so good a cause as yours."

"Then you agree with what I do," said Lann.

"I did not say that," Chando answered him. "For you may be breaking the hearts of the two people I love best in the world. Besides yourself, that is."

"My mother's heart is stronger than all that," said Lann.

"Perhaps you are right," Chando replied. "Though what son has ever *really* known his mother's heart. Still, I did not come down here so early just to chatter idly with you. Nor did I come to persuade you from your quest."

"Then why do you sit here, friend Chando?" asked Lann.

"To give you a parting gift," the minstrel replied. And he handed his golden lute to the boy.

Lann took the lute carefully. He passed his fingers lovingly over the neck, which was inlaid with ivory, and over the sound box, which had ivory flowers around the rosette. Then he held it back to Chando. "You cannot give me your lute," he said. "It is enough that you loaned it to me to practice on, these past six years."

"I *can* give it to you. Indeed, I *have* given it to you. For a man who is traveling needs a friend with him. And if he is a minstrel as you are, what better friend than his own lute."

"But what will you . . . ?"

"My young friend, my almost-son, I will have much quiet sitting time to make yet another. My traveling days are done. But you shall be too busy questing to carve and shape a lute for yourself. And on your safe return, we shall exchange. I shall give you the one I have worked upon for the year, and you shall give me back my own lute, well seasoned with travel."

A tear began to well up in Lann's eye.

"Nay, do not cry. For a man bent on questing has no time for tears," said Chando.

"A man always has time for tears," said Lann. "Thus my mother has always told me when I have cried and been teased for it. She says tears cannot unmake a man. They only prove that he loves well."

"Your mother is the wisest woman I know," said Chando, and clasped the boy to him so that Lann could not see the tears that fell unchecked from his eyes. "Go now, before I go with you." The minstrel walked off then, and did not look again at the boy.

Lann stood gazing up the strand. He said to himself, "But which way shall I go? South to the land of Cantwell, where men listen not and speak more than they know? Or west past the New Mountains to the home of the shepherds, where riches are counted in cattle and sheep? Or north, where men still live with the skins of animals untanned upon their backs? These are all lands I have heard of in song and story. Yet never have I heard of a crystal pool that 'from the salt sea springs.'"

Not knowing which way to start, Lann bent down and picked up a shell. For in Solatia, it was a game with the young boys and girls to toss a shell in the air and follow its point. "The shell compass," they said, "will take us to our pleasure."

Lann threw the shell high in the air. It made several turnings and came down. When it landed in the sand, its pointed end was toward the sea.

"Well, that is certainly not the choice I would have made," thought Lann. "For ship I have none. And that good a swimmer I am not." He bent down to pick up the shell to try again. As he stood up, he saw a movement far out on the sea. It was a shimmering that caught his eye. He wondered if it was fish or whale, and stood still for fully a minute. As he watched, a small rainbow formed where the sun touched the shimmer. Moments later, he saw what was causing it. It was a strange oval boat coming toward him, of mottled green. It had neither captain nor crew and was big enough for five or six as tall as he. When it came closer on the gentle tide, beaching soundlessly by his feet, Lann looked inside. There was no water in its well. At the bottom, half hidden under an oar, was a piece of cloth that looked to be a sail. The name carved on the boat's bow was "Song of the Sea."

"It is magic," thought Lann. "A song for a minstrel." And then he thought, "I wonder if it belongs to some poor shipwrecked soul." But he knew that no one in Solatia owned such a boat, for the design was strange to him and the writing most foreign.

Lann put the lute and his pack into the boat's well, and took off his boots and threw them in, too. Then he pushed the boat off the Solatian shore and hopped into *Song of the Sea*.

5. The Solatian Isles

Lann poled the boat away from the strand until it was free of the tide that moved ceaselessly toward the shore. Then he pulled the oar in and bent to the task of raising the sail. It was hard work, for a stiff breeze was blowing and at each try the wind threatened to tear the sail from his hands. But at last he was able to raise it, and without even benefit of her rudder, *Song of the Sea* headed joyously out toward the Solatian Isles.

He sat down in the boat's stern then and tried his hand on the rudder. He lifted his face and smelled the breeze. It looked to be a fine start to an adventure.

Lann felt new, or at least different from the way he had felt earlier in the morning. "It must be the boat," he thought. Though his great-grandfather had been a fisherman, Lann had never sailed this far from shore. Yet something sang in his body. And then he knew it was not the boat. It was the sea. Without even thinking, he began a song for the sheer joy of it:

> *"I seek you in silence,*
> *I seek you in singing,*

I seek you in sorrow,
I seek you in joy.

I seek you by asking,
I seek you by giving,
I seek you as man and
I seek you as boy."

And his song was like a shout and a prayer.

Suddenly, close by, he saw the nearest of the Solatian Isles, the Inner Isles. He guided the boat carefully into a narrow cove and marveled at the ease of it. "As if I had always been a sailor," he thought. And then again remembering his great-grandfather, he thought of it no more.

But when he stood on the shore and looked around, it seemed to be merely an extension of the land he knew so well. There were a few small cottages built like the ones on the Solatian shore, for often Solatians gathered here for special events: a wedding party or a time of fasting or for periods of silent thinking before a declaration of war.

Sadly Lann got back into the boat. Surely if the crystal pool were so close, he would have heard of it.

No sooner did he step into the boat than it seemed to take off by itself, as if it had a life of its own. He had neither to push it off with the oar nor steer it with the rudder. And they headed, for by now Lann thought of the boat as a person, toward the next of the Solatian Isles—the Mean Isles.

Lann had known of the Mean Isles for as long as he could remember. "Not because they are wicked," his grandfather Sian had told him when one day he asked, "but because they are in the middle, the mean." He could see clearly now what his grandfather had meant. In between Solatia and the Inner Isles on the one hand, and the Triades and the Outermost Isle on the other, nestled the Mean Isles.

They were but a waystop for fishermen, a place to dry the catch. Lann could see the wooden racks all along the shores of the many small isles. He merely shrugged, and the boat sped by.

As they neared the Triades, the three small isles that grouped together, Lann stood up in the boat, steadying himself with his hand on the mast. He cast a hurried glance at the three, but they were barren save for the bleached bones of an old ship lost many years back. It rested on the largest isle like a kit on its mother's breast. The wreck was picked clean, as clean as the Triades of growth. "Surely," thought Lann, "a crystal pool would mean trees nearby." He steered the boat around the three and past them.

When the Outermost Isle came into sight, some time later, a small oval isle with a groove in one side which some called a cove, Lann felt a chill. There the seawitch, Dread Mary, had made her home. Lann knew that the seawitch had saved his mother's life and taught her all her spells in exchange for the Solatian songs. So she must have been a good witch, regardless of all the bad tales they told about her.

"Still, if there is any crystal pool on that small isle, my mother would have known," he said aloud, as if addressing the boat.

And despite a rude rudder that did not want to listen to his hand and tried to steer itself straight toward the Outermost Isle, Lann put the boat's nose into the wind and sailed her out toward the open sea.

"To the Crystal Pool!" he shouted into the wind, feeling very brave and fortunate. A sound came back to him, as if in answer, but it was only the wind returning his voice to him in cries and whispers and sibilant sounds.

So Lann spent a day and a night in his boat, *Song of the Sea*. He fed himself from his small pack. His mother had put in some bread and cheese, and he had added dried golden fruit from her winter stores and a flask of berry wine. To keep himself warm, Lann drank several draughts of the wine. He slept then, wrapped in his dreams and rocked to sleep by the waves.

When he woke in the morn, the boat was caught on the edge of a strange green isle as if it were moored.

Lann stood up and rubbed sleep from his eyes, then he stretched and looked around. The isle was small and dome-shaped, and the ground seemed smooth and spread with moss. Lann slung his lute across one shoulder, the pack across the other, and stepped ashore. The ground was not smooth and mossy at all. It was slick and covered with a green slime. But by walking with care, Lann made his way to the top of the peak.

"'Tis odd," he thought when he stood upon it, "but the isle is the same on all sides like an egg. No coves, no grooves, no indentations."

Just as he made that observation, there was a rumbling and the entire island began to shake. Lann slipped and fell. But luck was with him, and he landed upon the pack of food and not upon the lute. When he was at last able to sit up again, he was shocked to find that the isle had grown a head and a tail.

"'Tis no isle at all but a giant turtle," he said to himself. He did not scream or call out, for doing so would have been useless. And like his mother and her father before her, he did not like to make useless cries for help.

"If it dives below the sea, I am a dead man," he thought. And added ruefully, "Though man I am not yet." Then he thought briefly about the button, the Magic Three, which he carried around his neck. He even put his hand on the chain. But when the tortoise, contrary to others of its kin, set to swimming above the waves with long leisurely pulls of its legs, Lann dropped the chain. He settled himself upon the island's peak, which was the uppermost part of the turtle's shell, and looked about.

The giant creature seemed not to notice him at all, and kept swimming in a northerly direction.

"Perhaps I had best get off while I can," Lann said to himself. But when he looked for his boat, he could just make it out on the horizon. And before he had time to blink again, the boat was out of sight.

"Well," he thought, "this monster is speeding faster than I thought. I wonder if I should try to swim?" But there was nothing but sea for miles around.

Lann looked down at the lute. "I wonder if it would float," he asked himself. He stroked the fine wood, not out of fear or even possessiveness, but with a kind of pity that he would not now have time to make its acquaintance. And then a sudden thought struck him. "There is nothing that happens that does not happen for a reason. Just as the shell pointed me to the boat and the boat brought me here, so perhaps this turtle will take me closer to my heart's desire. Who knows?"

So he settled himself more comfortably on the peak of the shell and took out his pack. He found he had squashed the cheese and bread by falling upon it, but still it was quite tasty. He ate the last of it. What was worse, though, was that he had lost his berry wine. It must have fallen down the turtle's back and slid into the sea when he slipped. The sun was now high in the sky, and there was nothing to shade him from it. He was becoming very thirsty, and thinking of thirst made him crave something to drink even more.

"Perhaps if I sing," he thought, "I shall forget my fears." So he put down the pack and picked up the lute, thinking to play a song.

But he had no time to begin, for just as he picked the instrument up, the turtle began to slow down. Lann stood up shakily. He put his hand above his eyes to shade them from the glare of the sky. Far ahead, but coming closer with each stroke of the turtle's powerful legs, was land.

6. Turtle Isle

The giant tortoise swam directly to the land. As they came closer, Lann could see it was a verdant isle with trees of every size and shape and much lush undergrowth. But of houses or boats, of roads or chapels or humankind, there was no sign.

There was a sudden bump as the turtle's feet touched shore. The giant did not stop, though, and continued directly upon the land, walking with the same rolling gait it had had in the sea.

"Enough for me," thought Lann. And, clutching his empty pack in one hand, the lute in the other, he slid down the back end of the turtle's shell and landed none too gracefully upon the shore.

He looked about him in wonder. The island seemed to creep and crawl with every manner of tortoise. There were small turtles with patterned shells and turtles whose backs were seamed and leathery. There were green turtles and brown turtles and yellow turtles and turtles with vermilion designs. There were turtles as small as Lann's smallest finger and some nearly as big as a horse.

Yet strange to say, for all the movement in the under-growth as the turtles moved slowly and clumsily onto the well-worn paths of the isle, there was no sound of life but the sound of a hiss.

As Lann watched, the giant tortoise that had carried him to the isle moved up a central pathway to a high peak. And when it reached the peak, where surely it must have been seen by the entire island, it raised its monstrous head to the sky and opened and shut its terrible jaws. The loud snap-snap resounded all over the isle.

As if at a signal, the turtles began to converge on Lann. Slowly, ponderously, but relentlessly, they came from all sides to the beach where he was standing. And before he could think of a plan of escape, he found himself surrounded by hundreds of turtles, their black, beady eyes staring at him, their mouths opening and shutting in imitation of their leader. But the only sound that emerged was that ever-present hiss.

Lann felt cold, yet warm too, as if his body could not catch up to his fears. He could barely move. Was this, then, the end of his quest?

As he pondered his fate, one especially large turtle pushed menacingly toward him and Lann stepped back awkwardly. As he moved, his elbow knocked the lute and set the strings a-quivering. At the strange new sound, the turtles all looked up and then down in a single motion, and stopped all move-ment as the sound of the humming strings died slowly in the air. When the sound could no longer be heard, the turtles began to move again.

"So that is the way of it," thought Lann. And he swung the lute in front of him and began to pluck a tune. As each note sang across the island, the turtles began to bob their heads on wrinkled necks up and down as if dancing. And soon Lann's fears subsided and he began to sing:

"The magic of a single song
Is but, in fact, a moment long.
But captured in your reverie,
That moment can forever be.
And so I sing a magic spell,
And hope I sing that moment well,
So my sweet song can catch you fast,
And in your heart forever last."

As the final notes hung in the air, sweet and simple and achingly pure, the turtles began to move. But not again in a menacing manner or toward Lann. Rather, many turned off and went toward the farther end of the isle. Lann heard an enormous splash and guessed that the giant tortoise had dived back into the sea. At that moment, a vermilion-colored turtle, about the size of a small dog, came slowly, majestically toward Lann, and laid its head on his boot. He bent down and scratched the creature's underjaw.

"I see," said Lann, with more than a little relief in his voice, "that we are now all friends."

Before long, the turtles were hurrying to the young minstrel with offerings, gifts of food, familiar-looking berries that he ate greedily and strange-looking plants he dared not try. One turtle even brought a broken eggshell. The halves were hard and leathery, and Lann soon discovered he could use them as a cup and bowl.

So Lann spent the rest of the day and the night at Turtle Isle, as he called it. He roamed over the isle and found one small muddy salt-free pool from which he could drink. It was as close as he came to finding a crystal pool. "But," he thought to himself, "not nearly close enough."

The turtles remained friendly enough, except for the monster, which Lann could occasionally see swimming far offshore and snapping its beak as if it were guarding the island. But after a while, Lann grew bored. The turtles could not talk or sing. All they could manage was a hiss. He would have to find a way off the isle in order to fulfill his pledge.

But he had no tools. Without tools, he could not make a boat. Without a boat, how could he escape the isle? The more he thought, the more hopeless he felt. And suddenly, all at once, Lann was overcome with grief. He remembered how brave and strong he had felt when he made his vow at the Thrittem, and that served to make him unhappier still. And when he thought of his mother saying "There comes a time when a boy and his mother must part," he put his head in his hands and began to weep loudly. It had been only two days ago. It seemed like years.

"Oh Mother, oh Grandfather, oh friend Chando," he cried out in a shaky voice, "that I were with you now." Then he reached inside his shirt and brought out the Magic Three and looked at it thoughtfully.

Just as he did, from far off on the other side of the isle he heard a clear, crystalline voice singing.

7. The Singer

Lann leaped up. "Another voice," he said aloud. The familiar words of the song bore down on him. It was the tune he had sung the day before, "The Magic Song." It was so good hearing a human voice again instead of that infernal hissing! He quickly tucked the Magic Three back into his shirt and vowed to find the owner of that voice. On such a small isle, it should not be so difficult a task.

Lann slung the lute upon his back and started up. The voice was singing still, the same song over and over. He followed it around the isle. The isle was not much larger than the village where Lann had lived, and in a single day he had gotten to know it well. It was shaped somewhat like a turtle, which had not surprised him. It was high in the middle, with four spits of sandy beach that jutted, like legs, into the sea. Where the head should have been was a cliff with an undersea grotto, as though the turtle isle had brought its head back into its shell. Lann had swum into the grotto, guided by his turtle companions, the day before. There was no tail to the island at all.

It was toward the place where the tail should have been

that Lann set off, for from there he was sure the voice was coming.

Just as he rounded the curve in the isle where he thought to find the singer, the music stopped.

"Sing on," he cried out. "Sing on, and I shall come to you."

But there was only silence, except for the constant hiss.

Lann swung his lute in front of him and began the first notes of "The Magic Song." As he had hoped, the notes from the lute coaxed the singer. The high pure voice sang the song again. But it was then that Lann understood what had been bothering him about the singer. The voice was like an echo, without change or emphasis. It sang the song as he had sung it. Not a note, not a word was wrong, but neither was there anything individual and new. Chando had always told him that it was important for the singer to bring something of his own to a song.

Lann followed the bodyless voice to a small willow tree. Then, at the foot of the tree, where buds beaded the branches like a rosary, he found a tiny turtle no bigger than his palm. Its back was studded with pearls that looked to be newly plucked from the sea. There was a tiny pearl crown upon its head. The turtle's tiny beak was open—and it was singing.

Lann's disappointment was so great that he flung himself to the ground beside it. He put his hand on its shell. "Little turtle," he said, "why, oh, why are you not of humankind?"

The turtle stopped singing and, strange to say, began to weep.

It was then that Lann noticed his own hand upon the turtle's pearly shell. He lifted his fingers to his face and stared. Surely he was mistaken. Yet as he looked more closely, he could see that his skin was becoming rough and scaly. And in between the fingers, where the skin is thinnest, was the faintest tint of green.

"I am becoming turtle," he said. He said it not with fear or even surprise, but with a kind of resignation, as though he had already suspected it long before.

8. The Shellboat

Lann must have lain next to the turtle for a long time, thinking or dreaming, it was hard to say which. One or two times his hand had strayed to the chain around his neck. Yet each time the memory of his mother's words, "Its consequences may be too hard to bear," stopped him from using the Magic Three. He could not imagine what consequences could be harder to bear than remaining here as a turtle on Turtle Isle. Yet the remembered pain in his mother's voice made him pause.

Finally he came to a decision. "I shall *have* to make a boat. Or swim if I must. But get off this island I will!" How different he felt from an hour ago, when he had collapsed in a miserable mound of tears. He was not sure what made him so determined, except that he had come to the end of all of the paths. Of that he was sure. If he could not find or make a boat, he would use the button.

So he got up and left the lute where it lay by the willow. He would need to be unencumbered for his task. In his mind's eye he drew a picture of the isle and divided it into sections. He determined he would search the isle methodically, step by step, to find something of use for his plan to escape. If he was certain there was no other way . . . well, he would have to bear those very consequences his mother so dreaded.

And so he began.

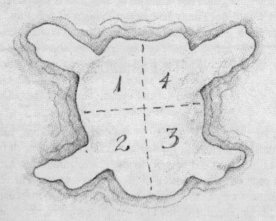

He searched each quadrant with care. He began with the beachside up and down. He progressed to the undergrowth that grew low and thickety, then up upon the hilly peak till he reached the top. But though he found small sticks and limbs abundantly upon the ground, they were not strong enough for a raft. And there was no way that he could see to bring down a mighty tree and hollow it out.

He was on the fourth fruitless journey up the side of the hill when he stumbled on something half hidden in a hole in the ground. He bent down and dug around it with his hands. Slowly he unearthed it. It was the shell of a turtle more than twice his own size. It was a mottled green-brown and reminded him of something.

"Why, of course," he said out loud. "It looks just like *Song of the Sea*, only smaller. I can use it as a boat." He dug it out of the ground where it had lain hollow down, and turned it over.

The insides were clean as if scoured by beetles, and smoothly rounded. Having no tools, he could make no mast. But surely he could use branches as oars. It was not perfect, but it would do. Funny he had not thought of it before.

So Lann pushed the shell before him and started down toward the beach. But, coming upon the shore, he saw swimming toward him the giant turtle, no longer on patrol. It had somehow sensed his plans for escape. It pulled with its mighty legs and moved through the water at incredible speed. Its head was up and snapping as it came.

Lann had one thought then, to run. But he needed the shellboat in order to escape. So he hoisted it upon his back and began to climb the hill again, away from the monster that was approaching the isle.

He could hear the turtle behind him as it came ashore. Its lumbering gait upon the beach, its loud hiss and snap-snap filled his ears. The shell upon his back grew heavier and heavier with each step. He could feel his neck and arms grow sweaty and the shell pressing down, sticking to his shoulders. He had an awful urge to fall upon his knees and crawl the rest of the way to the top, but he fought the urge. Just then he reached the peak.

Barely taking time to look behind him, where he knew the monster was gaining at every step, Lann threw the shell upside down onto the ground. He could feel it rip his shirt and swore his own skin had come away from his back almost as though it had become attached to the shell. He pushed the shell down the slope and jumped into it. It slid easily along the well-worn path, gathering speed as it went. The giant tortoise was soon far behind.

The shell cannoned into the water with a loud splash. As Lann looked behind him, he saw the giant tortoise creeping down the hill toward the shore.

In the water, Lann saw his lute floating in the shellboat's wake. On top of the lute, near the neck, was the pearly turtle, paddling with its front legs as if in a boat.

Lann leaned over and grabbed up the ruined lute and the turtle. As he did so, he noticed that his hand on the lute's slim neck was no longer rough and scaly. The green that had been between his fingers was gone. He felt relieved but not surprised.

"Come, little friend, and welcome," Lann said to the turtle. "I see my lute is ruined for play. So let us put it to work instead."

Placing the turtle beside him in the boat, he picked up Chando's golden lute. He glanced at his hand again and, with a smile, he put the lute's body into the sea.

"Row on," he said to encourage himself, and began to paddle as fast as he was able.

9. Ail'issa

They had gone but a little way when the giant tortoise slid with an enormous splash into the sea and started after them.

Lann pulled on the lute paddle with all his might, but there seemed no way they could escape. The giant came closer, swimming as no other turtle swims and snapping its jaws angrily as it came.

Lann thought desperately of the Magic Three, yet he determined to try one more thing. He remembered how the turtles had responded to his singing before. If he could sing, and sing loudly, paddling all the while, perhaps he could tame—or at least slow down—the fearsome beast.

He wondered quickly what he might sing, then decided to sing *all* the songs he knew. And since he had so recently sung them and knew them well, he began with his Thrittem songs, "Come Make Me Man" and "A Year of Growing." As he sang, the giant turtle slowed down and stopped snapping its jaws, swimming silently around the boat as if waiting for the spell to end.

Lann finished each song and began another with the same breath. He sang the seven gypsy songs his mother Sianna loved. He sang all the songs that Chando sang so well:

songs of love gained and love lost and love never found. He sang of spring blossoms and winter snow, of western winds and eastern rains. And when he had finished all the songs that sprang from the farming people, he sang the chapel songs as well. He sang the Seven Psalms of Waking and the songs in praise of silence, which was ever the Solatian way. Then he began the songs of the sea, but by this time his voice was nearly a croak. The sun straight up in the sky burning down into his turtle boat was making him mad with thirst. He paddled more slowly with each passing hour.

And all the while, the giant turtle swam about the boat, its head high out of the water. Its black eyes, as large as darkened windows, were angry. But it made no threatening move.

Lann continued to sing in his ruined voice, watching the giant with slight hope. But feeling his voice failing, he began to sing especially to the little turtle beside him in the boat, a song he made up to an old tune:

> *"Little one, our time has come.*
> *There are no more songs to be sung.*
> *My voice is cracked, my throat is numb,*
> *I feel no movement in my tongue.*
>
> *So if you can, please add a note,*
> *And lift your voice to aid our case.*
> *Take pity on my weakened throat,*
> *Or else right here we end our race."*

But the little turtle did not reply. And Lann, singing and paddling still, turned his head to see why. In the bottom of the boat, the little turtle lay as if dead, its shell cracked open from the blazing sun.

"Oh, friend," cried Lann, dropping the lute in the water

and picking up the tiny creature. He began to weep then, partly for himself, but also for the turtle whose death he thought he had caused. As he cried, he stopped singing and the giant tortoise snapped its mighty jaws and came toward them. It raised its head and brought it down angrily upon the lute again and again. The lute was shattered into hundreds of pieces.

But Lann, still weeping, seemed not to hear, though the small boat tossed madly with the fury of the waves. The tears came twinkling down from his eyes and landed upon the cracked shell of the tiny turtle. As they fell, they soothed the broken carapace. And while Lann watched, the water from his eyes began to shimmer and glow on the turtle's back. The shell came apart in his hands, and he placed the tiny turtle without its shell on the bottom of the boat trying to shade it with his hand. But a strange thing occurred. The turtle began to grow and change. Its beak and scaly skin sloughed off, and before Lann's wondering eyes it grew into a tall, slim, green-skinned woman with a pearl crown, a green mantle, and a short green kirtle beaded with pearls. The woman had a grim look on her face as she ripped the crown from her sea-green hair and flung it at the monster.

The giant tortoise saw the pearly crown sail through the air. It raised its massive head and snapped at the delicate crown with its beak. It seemed a miracle that it caught the crown without crushing it. Then the giant sank like a stone and did not come up again.

Only then did the green-haired woman turn to Lann. "Come, my brave lad," she said. And when she smiled at him he thought her teeth were as white as the pearls on her dress. "Let us row to my country. It is not so far that we cannot bend ourselves to the task. It is called Iss, and I am Ail'issa, its queen."

10. Ail'issa's Tale

As they paddled along with their hands, Ail'issa told Lann her story. It was as strange as she.

"I am descended from the great turtles of long ago, and so are my people," she said. "We are seafarers and plow the waters of the world in turtleshell boats. We fish for our food and dive for pearls, which we use in trade, and we live a happy life by the grace of the sea.

"But we are not the only great-grandchildren many times removed of those ancient turtles. For, many thousands of years ago, the turtle clan made a branching. One half took the road to manhood, one half remained great tortoises. One half knew singing and laughter, one half knew hissing and grief. And the turtle crown, the pearl of great price, was given to my people.

"So the giant tortoises grew angry. For many hundreds of years there has been a war between their kind and ours. The pearl crown has been won and lost many times over.

"For thousands of our years, which is as one in theirs, the giant tortoise you have seen has been the ruler. Slysyth is his name, and he is twisted and evil and hates all of us who can walk upright upon land.

136

"But thirteen years ago, foul number, Slysyth established a magic isle in the middle of our waters with the help of a wizard cast out from his own land. Upon that isle, a man is condemned to walk as a turtle, house on his back, and creep about with no speech save a hiss. In exchange for his help in creating the isle, the unknown wizard learned from Slysyth the magic of change, how to make man a beast. For that is ever Slysyth's way, to bring us, who have moved away from the beast's dumb ways, back to the ground.

"Now one day, when I and my sailors were skimming the sea in my boat, we beached upon Slysyth's broad back and were carried off to Turtle Isle, where we were as you found us. And my ship, *Song of the Sea*, was seen no more."

"But I have seen it," cried Lann, interrupting the flow of her tale. "I have ridden in it. I was in it when I, too, ran aground upon the green back of that beast."

"Why, then," said Ail'issa, "that explains how you came to the isle. For never had I known Slysyth to strike at other than my own folk. If you were in my boat, he thought you of my kind."

"So that is why I was not immediately turned to turtle," said Lann. "Because I was not of turtle kind."

"But eventually you would have changed. Longer it might have taken, but the power of change cannot be stayed as long as one remains on Turtle Isle."

"How came you, of all your people, to retain your voice?" asked Lann.

"It was my crown," replied the queen. "Surely you guessed that."

Lann had to admit he had not. And to himself he said, "There is still much more to magic than one of thirteen can know."

"The sea crown saved me my voice, though I could not sing my own words. I could only repeat what else was said. And since before you came there was naught to repeat but a hiss, that was all that I could do."

Lann smiled then, remembering the curious echo quality
in the singing voice that had bothered him. "So when I came
and sang, I tamed the beasts. Such my mother had often
said was the power of song. I thought it but a tale."

"She must surely be a wise woman," said the queen.

"She is the wisest woman I know," Lann replied, then
realizing he was in the company of another woman, he
blushed.

Ail'issa laughed. "You have little experience with women,
I see. Nor with queens either, I would guess. But do not
fear, I am not angry with such a loving statement. Surely
not from the lad who has saved my life."

"I have saved your life, perhaps," said Lann. "But I have
lost you your crown."

"Nay, little friend, *you* have not lost my crown. *I* have
lost it. For to effect our escape, it was necessary to throw
it to Slysyth. He was more than satisfied with the exchange.
But never mind, what has been lost can be again found.
And indeed, Slysyth does not know what a prize he has
lost. For like the animal he is, he does not see farther than
the ground. Before I escaped this isle, no one had known
of its existence and we could but guess at what had become
of our ships lost at sea. My own father, King L'iss himself,
lies imprisoned on that isle in a vermilion shell. And one
day soon I shall find a means to rescue him. Till then, let
us row, you and I, to my land, which lies not far from here,
I think. And then my own sailors shall bring you home
again."

"But I cannot go home as yet," cried Lann.

"What, so young and yet parted from your so-wise mother
by your own choosing?" asked Queen Ail'issa. "In our land
it is not ever so."

And so it was that Lann told her his tale, of his mother
and his grandfather, of the overheard spell and the Thrittem

pledge. And when he was done, Ail'issa looked quite thoughtful.

"My sailors have seen the seventeen seas and all the lands hereabout. If there is such a pool that from a salt sea springs, they shall know of it or they shall find it. And *I* shall save your grandfather as you have saved me."

So they set to rowing with their hands and came, after three more days, hungry and thirsty and half dead from the sun, to the coast of the land of Iss.

11. The Crystal Pool

The land of Iss was strange and beautiful in Lann's eyes. For though in Solatia much was owed to the sea, in Iss the sea itself seemed to have invaded the land. Houses were built of green bricks made of seaweed, with mosses lining the cracks. Sea buds and sea blossoms were on every shelf. Fish was served at each meal. And the tall green-skinned women and their tall green-skinned men spent fully half their lives in the sea, swimming or diving for pearls or sailing far off alone or in pairs in their turtleshell boats.

Lann had not been there half a year when he began to worry about his vow, and to grow weary of the endless tales the sea-colored Issians told. For they were a race devoted to long stories, the points of which were most often lost on the lad.

At first Lann had been delighted with the strange new ways of the seafolk and had hoped to find the crystal pool in one of their tales. But now he grew despondent. It was as if a scant two seasons had aged him a hundred years.

By guestrite, Lann had been forced each day to sit the morning by Ail'issa's side and listen to the returning sailors spin out their yarns over large draughts of brine-flavored wine. The wine was sour to Lann's taste, and so, at last, were the tales. And if the women sailors were more or less boring than the men, Lann could not tell, for they had become the same to him.

"My Lady Ail'issa," Lann said at last one morn when another Issian sailor had been about to begin his tale, "I do not mean disrespect to your folk. But I have been here both summer and fall, and still have not begun my search for the crystal pool. I do not see the point of sitting here and telling tales and taking no action at all."

Ail'issa laughed and clapped her hands then, and the sailor, who had been standing, sat before them, his legs folded under him, waiting for the signal to begin.

"My young friend Lann," she replied, "if there is one thing my people know, it is the long patience of the sea. The sea rolls in each day and rolls out each night and never wearies of this, its ancient role. Perhaps this is the difference between your people and mine. But I think it is rather the difference between the young and the old. You must learn that to hurry is not necessarily to hasten."

"But to do nothing at all is neither," complained Lann. "And now I have less than half a year to save my grandfather."

"Do you think that what we do here is nothing?" asked Ail'issa. Her voice was not hard or threatening, indeed there was a teasing laugh in it.

Lann nodded miserably. Then he softened his words. "At least, I do not see the use of it."

"My sailors have been the world over," Ail'issa said. "Or at least the world where it is touched by the sea. And each man returns with knowledge which, though it may seem unworthy to your mind, serves to enlarge our books. For with such tales, the books of knowledge are made larger and the world is made smaller. And with each new friend found, the world is brought home."

Lann thought about what she said. Then at last he spoke. "I think you are as wise as my mother," he said.

"Well, perhaps we are both wise in different ways." And she signaled for the man to speak.

This sailor was more brown than green, which Lann knew was a sign of age. His sea-green eyes were slightly faded, as when the sea is seen through fog. He was smaller than most Issians Lann had met, but wiry and looked very strong.

"My queen, I am Syss, of the Cyth clan. My trip is of little worth. I sailed many days to the south and east of here in a single boat. There I found a group of islands strung out like broken pearls on a chain. Of the other isles, cruised by fishermen and blasted by the sun, I have nothing to say. But of one, where I stayed a day and a night, I speak.

"This isle was small, but a droplet in the sea. Oval in shape, it had a deep groove in one side that served as a cove. And naught was on it but a copse of trees and a pool. Yet you said, be ware of pools. So I stayed.

"Of the pool, know this, it is crystal and the water pure. No sea fish or sea creature can live in it. Yet by its very side lie the bones of a giant fish. Yet no fish at all that I can tell, rather a great fishtail. There is a golden bird that circles the pool and drinks from it but once a day. And when it is finished drinking, it sings a song that goes like this." And here Syss pursed his lips and let out a call that sounded like *"Sia, sia, sia, sia."* Lann and Ail'issa and then Syss himself set to laughing so hard that it was fully a minute till they recovered.

Syss looked serious again and ended, "My queen, it seemed then and now of little worth. Yet because of the pool, so crystal and pure, I hurried back to tell of it instead of going on."

"You did well, my friend," said Ail'issa. "And now you may go."

"Wait!" cried Lann. "This golden bird. Was it, perchance a *Gard-lann,* a king-lark?"

"Such a bird I have never seen," said Syss. "What is a lark? I know naught of birds and what they be called elsewhere. Ask me of the sea."

"But if this is perhaps a lark, and a golden one, then it is perhaps the *Gard-lann* after which I was named," said the lad excitedly. He turned to the queen. "Dear Ail'issa, surely there cannot be another such in the world. And if this crystal pool has a fishtail by, perhaps it is from that salt-sea fish that it springs."

"Nay, little man," said Syss. "The pool does not spring from the tail. Of that I am sure. They lie close together. That is all."

"But perhaps..." began Lann.

"There are too many perhapses in this tale," said Ail'issa. "You must be patient and it will come aright. Or if it does not, then it was not meant to be."

"You are wise, my royal friend," said Lann, "but my mother is wise, too. And she has oft repeated to me a Solatian saying, 'There is a time of dreaming and a time of doing.' That time, I think, has come. Sailor Syss, show me the way to this isle."

Syss looked questioningly at the queen.

"Show him," she commanded. "A man must do as he will."

And so Lann and Syss got in one of the turtleshell boats, and Syss rigged it with a sail. They packed plenty of provisions for the trip and set off by the stars, for so it was done in the land of Iss. And within a large number of days, they came close by an isle that seemed but a droplet in the sea.

"That, young master, is the isle," said Syss.

"But," said Lann, unable to keep the disappointment from his voice, "I know that isle. It is the Outermost Isle, I am sure." He looked closely at the small island, then off a short distance at a group of three islands nearly touching one another. Farther on was a ridge of mountainous isles. And farther still, yet another group. And then a long, sweeping coast.

"Does it matter?" said the sailor. "To recognize something is not necessarily to know it. And often what we seek for far away has always been close at hand. It is only distance that lends perspective."

Lann sighed and nodded then, and climbed out of the turtle boat. Syss would have come with him, but Lann signaled him to stay and waded ashore alone. "I must do this myself," he called over his shoulder.

So Lann walked along the strand that sparkled with familiar iridescent shells. Presently he came to a small pool. He looked down into its depths and could see all the way to the bottom.

Lann plunged his hand into the pool and brought the water to his lips. It was as cold and pure as Syss had said. Lann drank it greedily. Then he walked around the side of the pool and there, as the sailor had told, was a giant fishtail, its scales still shimmering in the light of the sun and making rainbows on the sand. Lann bent down to pick it up and as he touched it, it crumpled into dust. At that very moment, a golden bird came out of the trees and flew once around Lann's head singing, "*Sia, sia, sia.*" Then it settled on his shoulder and would not fly off again, even when he stood up.

"I do not know how this pool came here," Lann said aloud, "except that it has somewhat to do with the fish's tail. But if I were to guess from the stories my mother told me, I would guess that this is the doing of the seawitch, Dread Mary. And if she had aught to do with it, it springs from the salt sea." Saying this, Lann plunged his shell flask into the pool and brought it up full. Then he capped it with care and, the bird still riding his shoulder, walked back to the boat.

12. And After

And so Lann and his sailor friend Syss came to the Solatian shore. When Lann stepped onto the shining strand, the children playing there recognized him at once and ran to tell Sianna of her son's return.

They bathed Sian in the pure crystal water and slowly, over the months, feeling returned to his limbs. Though he was not a young man again, he could walk and move with ease. And his constant companion was the golden bird, which could now say *"Sian, Sian, Sian."*

When Lann tried to return the Magic Three to his mother, Sianna said, "You have used it more wisely than I."

"But I did not use it at all," replied Lann.

"That is what I mean," said Sianna. "And so you shall keep it. For someday you may have need of it. I think I shall have no more."

At the end of that year, in a small ceremony at the chapel, Lann was called man. Chando gave him yet another lute. "But use this one to sing with, not to paddle," he cautioned.

Then Lann sat down in the chapel and began to play. If he noticed his mother and Chando walking out the door, their arms around one another, her head resting lightly on his broad chest, Lann did not disapprove. For now that his grandfather had returned to health and now that he was himself a man, it was a time of new freedom for him. And he knew it was his mother's time as well.

Here ends Book III

BOOK IV

Wild Goose and Gander

Book IV is for Jason

Contents: Book IV

Before

When a man comes to be twenty years old, it is time to leave his mother's house. At least, that is what is said in Solatia, a land of much greenness and harvest gold.

So it happened that Lann, a minstrel untried in his songs except among his neighbors and friends, decided to do more than leave his mother's house. He decided to leave her land as well.

"And if I find fortune or fame, it is fine," he said. "But more, I should like to travel to all the lands both near and far, and even to the back of beyond, to seek what I know not. To sing I know not what. And to call many 'friend' along the way."

So his mother, Sianna, blessed him and gave him an amulet to wear on his breast. But when he was but a little way off, he placed the stone in his pack, for sometimes a man wants to try his own magic without his mother's aid. And Lann had faith in the power of his songs, for there is a kind of magic in music as well.

Besides, if truth be known, Lann had a chain around his neck on which there hung a button. It held magic so powerful that it had never been used. For magic has consequences, this Lann knew. Yet he knew, too, that if sometime a terrible need arose, those consequences, no matter how dear, would have to be borne.

And so Lann traveled, lute on his back, out into the wide wide world.

1. Wild Goose and Gander

In a forest at the back of the world lived a brother and sister. By day they were wild geese and soared in the sky high above the tops of the tallest trees. But at night they flew back to their forest hut and in human form dined on red berries, green salad, and wine.

They had no one but each other, and it had been so from the first. They had been left in the forest by their frightened nursemaid on the day after they were born. For in the evening they had been babies wrapped in swaddling, but in the daylight they turned into soft-feathered goslings in the folds.

The wizard who had changed them was named Bleakard. He lived in a gray-green stone castle perched high on a mountain crag that rose in the middle of a lake. Each day he summoned the brother and sister to his castle with a magic flute. They were forced to fly away from their forest hut and circle the mountaintop. As day closed, he would let them go, and they winged home with fear-filled speed.

So the brother and sister lived in the forest at the back of beyond with one another as company and no one else in the whole wide world to call a friend.

Late one afternoon, into the forest came the young minstrel Lann. He had been gone from his home a year and a day and had spent each night under a different roof.

When he saw the forest hut covered with wild goose grasses, he smiled. He was tired, and it seemed a likely place to stop. So he laid his lute against the wall and tapped lightly on the door. When no one answered, he pushed the door open and went in.

Inside he saw two beds neatly made and a table neatly set for two. He saw two wardrobes filled with clothes and two stone basins brimming full. But no one was there to greet him.

"I shall wait for the owners to return," thought Lann, and settled himself outside on the ground by the door. He was so weary from traveling that he soon was fast asleep.

Scarcely had he dozed off than a great whirring filled the air, the sounds of wings beating. Two shadows fell upon the minstrel's sleeping form. A wild goose and gander sailed down from the skies and landed at his feet.

At once they changed to human form. The brother, a tall lad, was named Bred, with eyes so black they seemed to have no bottom. The sister was named Bridda. Her hair was soft as feathers, her face as gentle as the wind.

Bridda clung to her brother when she saw the sleeping stranger. But Bred was more courageous and put out his hand.

"Awake, friend, and welcome," he said, as the minstrel opened his eyes.

"I did not hear you come," said Lann, jumping up. "I beg your pardon..."

"It is no matter," Bred replied, and led the way into the house.

Because they had only two dishes and two cups, Bred had to wait until the minstrel finished his meal. And because the minstrel tuned his lute and sang one song after another to the smiling Bridda, Bred finished his dinner alone.

When the dishes were washed and carefully set aside for the morning, Bred joined his sister and the minstrel outside under the trees and they talked and sang until almost dawn.

Just before the sun rose, the minstrel fell into a dreamless sleep. And when the sun had fully lit the path to the hut, Bred and Bridda returned to the air. They circled once, and the goose cast a sad backward glance at the sleeping man before she joined the gander in their wingtip-to-wingtip journey across the sky.

2. The Enchantment

That evening the goose and gander returned. As before, they touched the earth in front of the sleeping man. He was sunk again in a magical sleep so that he would not see them change.

When he awoke at last, Lann said to Bred, "This is most strange. I was asleep when you left and asleep when you returned. Yet I was not tired. There is some enchantment here that I do not understand."

"It is no matter," said Bred, and he led Lann into the house.

That evening the minstrel and Bridda ate in silence, watching each other with love-filled eyes. For Bridda had never seen another human, except her brother and the wizard. And Lann, though he had seen many maidens in his year of traveling, had never met one who so combined silence and singing, wisdom and beauty, shyness and courage.

And Bred was content to eat alone after them.

Then the three friends talked until dawn.

For three nights it was thus. But on the fourth night, before they settled down to talk, the minstrel took the stone charm from his saddlebag. He remembered what his mother had said when she had given it to him. "If you are ever in a land of strangers and strangeness, place this amulet upon your breast."

The minstrel placed the charm over his heart. And after breakfast, though he was not tired at all, he pretended to fall asleep.

Just as the sun came up, Bred and Bridda began to change. First their hair turned to feathers, then feathers soft and white grew on their arms. At last their bodies were covered with down. And as they beat their great wings, they were transformed entirely into giant birds that rose up into the air and set off past the sun.

That evening when the geese returned to their forest home, they found the minstrel awake and waiting.

"Am I dreaming still, or is this enchantment?" Lann asked them when they touched the ground and turned back into humans.

"It is enchantment," said Bred softly.

Bridda wept silently. She feared that the minstrel could not love a girl who was a bird by day.

"I know about spells as I know about singing, for my mother is Sianna of the Song. Perhaps you have heard of her. There must be a way I can help you," said the minstrel.

"There is no help for us," replied Bred. "We were transformed as babies by a wicked wizard. We were left here in the forest by our nursemaid and must return to the wizard's castle each day."

Bridda added, "We do not know our mother or our father. We only know what Bleakard, the wizard, has told us: That we fed as goslings and grew as children until we are as you see us now. And each day we must go and fly around the bleak rock castle to his tune."

Lann looked thoughtful. "And the spell?"

Bred said, "We do not know the spell. And if we do not

know the spell, how can we break it? We only know what we must do each day and how we must be each night."

Lann laughed. "If you can not break the spell, then you must break the spell maker. So my mother Sianna, who is the wisest person I know, taught me. And so I believe. I must go to the wizard who made this magic and wrest his secrets from him."

"Easier said than done," said Bridda. "The way leads through an enchanted forest and across a perilous lake."

"Better tried than not," replied Lann.

So in the morning, after a short nap, Lann started off. Inside his shirt he placed a feather that Bridda had plucked from her breast. It was still warm to the touch. He followed the only path through the wood while the wild goose and gander circled above as if to point the way.

3. Jared

It was day by the hut, but it was night in the woods. The way through the forest was long and cold and dark. The trees were hung with rags of fog.

As Lann walked along, his lute slung over his shoulder, the cold seemed like daggers of ice piercing his heart. And only where Bridda's feather touched him did he feel warm.

"Fear feeds on fear," thought he. So he unslung his lute, thinking to play a strengthening song. As each string was plucked and stretched, a small bit of light sparked the darkness.

"Aha," thought Lann, "so that is the way of it." And then, as if to reassure himself, but also to let any forest ears hear that he was not afraid, he repeated it out loud. "So that is the way of it."

And he began a cheery-sounding song which he made up as he walked along the midnight path. For minstrels are trained to sing a new song as easily as an old one.

> *"The way is dark, the path is long,*
> *And sometimes right begins as wrong.*
> *But I've found as I go along*
> *The world is warmed by just a song.*

And as I'm getting warmed a bit,
And gathering up my scattered wit,
I see a pattern, I'll admit,
By just a song the world is lit.

For song is warmth and song is light,
And song can pierce the darkest night.
My lute's my weapon in this fight,
And what is wrong can be set right.

The way is dark, the path is long,
And sometimes right begins as wrong.
But I've found as I go along
The world is warmed by just a song."

And he ended on a single high clear note.

As the song faded away like fireflies in a dark wood, winking and blinking and sparking and drifting at last into nothing, the forest was again dark. But now the dark seemed heavier and colder than before. Even the feather against his breast was cool.

Lann looked about him. "If this is the way of it," he thought, "I do not think I like the way." But he continued on, humming his tune and strumming occasionally on the lute to keep his fingers warm.

As he walked farther, Lann thought he heard another rhythm, a steady *one-two, one-two*. "Left foot, right foot," he said to himself. And soon he found his fingers playing that same steady beat on the strings. His own feet followed after, and he marched toward the sound.

As he marched on, Lann saw a small light ahead. Each step brought him nearer the light, and each step seemed to make the light bigger. Finally Lann could make out a large clearing, and the rhythmic pounding of the *one-two, one-*

two was now so loud that it made his ears ring.

Through the ringing in his ears, Lann thought he could hear a difference between the *one* and the *two*. The *one* was loud and crackling, like a fire or the breaking of trees and branches. The *two* was a softer, almost melodic swish, of wind through flowers.

When at last he came to the clearing, which was only a lighter shade of the forest dark, for the sky overhead was heavy and gray with forbidding clouds, Lann saw what was making the noise. It was a giant of a man in leather pants and a leather jerkin, with leather bands around his wrists. He was stomping left foot, right foot, left foot, right foot, round and round the forest clearing.

As the gigantic left foot came down, lightning and fire flashed from the toes. Smoke curled up where the giant stepped. The ground beneath his left foot turned sere and brown, and nothing living grew there again. But where his right foot descended, cooling rains fell from the arch. Flowers dropped from his foot onto the path and took root there.

"Ho there," called Lann as the giant's right foot came down once again.

The gigantic man stopped stomping and turned toward the sound. His voice, so rough and grating on the ear, made furrows in the air. "Who speaks?"

Lann played a chord on his lute. "It is I, Lann. A wandering minstrel."

The giant's rough face broke into a smile. "And I am Jared," he said. "It has been many years since I have had company."

"It is a far way to find your clearing, friend," said Lann pleasantly. "Perhaps that is why you have so few visitors. I only happened here myself. Why don't you come and meet the world?"

Jared frowned. He pointed despairingly at his feet.

"Wherever the one steps, I destroy. Wherever the other, I create. I can go nowhere without this double curse—flame and flowers, flowers and flame."

"Cursed," said Lann. It was a statement, but the giant heard a question and so replied.

"By Bleakard, the wizard. Once I was a king. And a rather foolish, cowardly king, I am afraid. But I loved to sing and dance and be entertained. My people rather enjoyed it, too. And they called me Jared the Good and said that flowers followed where I trod. But I trod once on a wizard's toes, I think. I thought him but a visiting magician and boasted of my own worth. That blackguard Bleakard laughed and said, 'So you create flower gardens in your path, do you?' and brought his magic flute down upon my feet. I suppose I fainted. For when I came to, I was here in the forest as you see me now. And here I have stayed, for I do not think I could face either my people or that wizard again."

"And what will end the spell?" asked Lann.

"I do not know," replied Jared. "I have told you all I know—of the spell and of my past. The rest seems to be lost to me, I know not why."

"If you cannot break the spell," said Lann, remembering when he said the same before, "you must break the spell maker."

"But I dare not," said Jared. "The shame of visiting my people. The fear of visiting Bleakard..."

Lann put his hand out and touched the giant's hand. "I am off to visit Bleakard myself. Why not come along with me? A friend is always a welcome companion in the dark. And your people would not think less of you as you are now."

"I dare not," whispered the giant. Yet his whisper was loud enough to bend the trees with its noise. "For I have just now recalled a part of the curse. Bleakard will kill me if I come to the castle."

"Is that any worse than living the way you are now?" asked Lann softly. "Going round in circles of fire and flowers?"

"I daren't," said the giant. "Here at least I am still a king. And I do not want to die." He looked as if he might weep.

"But I dare," said Lann. "And I am not afraid to die." He added "I think" under his breath, remembering Bridda.

The minstrel slung his lute over his back and crossed the clearing, over alternate stubbles of burned grass and patches of red and gold flowers. He started down the only path that led away from the clearing. Bridda's feather was again warm against his skin.

Lann had gone but four steps into the darkened forest when he heard a cry from behind. It sounded like a sigh, like a gulp, like a plea, like a song. It was the giant.

"Wait, oh wait, and I'll come too."

4. Coredderoc

Lann turned and waited. In a minute, trailing fire and flowers, Jared had run to his side.

Carefully Lann stepped around the giant to his right side. Then side by side, Lann taking two steps to the giant's one, they made their way deeper into the forest. But whereas before the forest had been dark and lit only by the notes that sang from Lann's lute, now it was blazing-bright from the flames from the giant's foot.

"You see," said Lann, "there is good in every bad. Sometimes right begins as wrong."

Jared shook his head as if trying to clear it. "I do not find your meaning," he said.

"I mean that if you were not *cursed*, we could not see. At least not so clearly. Your foot shall light our way to Bleakard's castle."

"Why didn't I think of that?" exclaimed Jared.

"That is what a friend is for," replied Lann. "To turn a liability into an ability."

"It sounds quite fine when you say it," said Jared. "But it is one of those matters to which I will have to give a lot of thought."

And so he did.

For a while neither of the new friends spoke, but walked on in silent companionship, accented only by the hissing of the flames and the twanging of the lute strings being tuned.

When at last the lute was tuned again—for lute strings need much attention, just as people do—Lann began a song especially for his new friend.

> "A friend is the other side of a coin,
> A friend is an old song resung.
> A friend is the other side of your moon,
> A friend is an old lute restrung.
>
> And if I never knew it before,
> I guess I know it today.
> And if I haven't said it before,
> Then this is the right time to say:
>
> A friend is just you turned inside out,
> A friend is yourself turned round.
> And nothing's as good in a darkling wood
> As a friend who's newly found."

Jared laughed then for the first time, and clapped Lann so hard on the back in his enthusiasm that Lann pitched forward into the dark and nearly smashed his lute upon a tree.

"Hold, friend Jared," the minstrel called out. "I appreciate your gesture but not your gusto. Take care. The lute and I can be equally unstrung."

At that Jared laughed again and promised to be gentler. And the two walked on singing Lann's new-made song together. For the giant, as he had claimed, enjoyed a song and his voice was pleasing, if a bit too loud.

They had gone but a mile or maybe three when they

heard the sound of fierce quarreling ahead. It was as if two men were screaming at one another at the top of their voices. Yet both voices were so similarly pitched that it was hard to distinguish one from the other.

"Hold, friend," said Lann. "I will sneak on ahead. For with your hissing and sparking, we will never creep up upon these battlers unawares."

"Nay, you hold, friend," replied Jared. "You are but a stripling and I am a giant of a man. What we lose in surprise we will gain in awe. For when these two fighters see me and my fiery foot, they will set to such a shaking and quaking that their bones will play a knocking to accompany your strings."

But much to the giant's relief, Lann would not hear of it. And so, after a few words more, the two decided to go on together, which is the way of friends.

Around a final bend in the road they could distinguish another clearing, smaller than the last. And when they had come to the road's ending and the grass's beginning, they saw the strangest sight either had ever seen.

Instead of two men quarreling in the meadow, there was but a single man, so small he could be nothing but a dwarf. Stranger yet, the dwarf had not one but two heads. And it was these two heads that were quarreling, the one with the other. They shouted, "I am," and "You are not, I am," back and forth at one another, snarling and gnashing teeth, sticking out tongues and spitting. It was a thoroughly disgusting exhibition.

"Ho there," called Lann and Jared together into one of the few silences.

The two heads turned toward the new voices at the same time. "Who speaks?" they said in unison.

"It is I, Lann, a wandering minstrel," said the lad, strumming a chord on his lute, which was sadly out of tune again.

"And I, Jared, who once was a mighty king," said the

giant, stomping his left foot down with such violence that the flames shot high into the air. Lann looked over at him, and Jared added, "Well, maybe not *so* mighty."

"And I am Coredderoc," said the head on the right.

"He is not, I am Coredderoc," said the head on the left.

"He is lying," said the first head. "I always tell the truth."

The second head spat at the first and missed. "He is the one who always lies, I am telling the truth."

Lann put his head to one side and thought a minute. "It puts me in mind of an old paradox," he said. "My mother taught it to me."

"No," said the first head. "You have it wrong. It is only a paradox if I say 'I always lie.'"

"And you do," added the second.

"I do not," said the first.

"Well, it matters not," said Lann pleasantly. "You both look equally like Coredderoc to me."

"It matters indeed," said the two heads together. "I am cursed. By the wicked wizard Bleakard, blast his black soul." Both heads turned aside and spat on the ground at the wizard's name. It seemed the only thing they could agree upon.

"Cursed?" said Jared loudly.

"Yes. Once I was a royal minister to a truly great king who had recently lost his wife in childbirth. Bleakard was but a visiting magician, or so I thought at first. But when first the queen died, bless her beautiful soul, and then the royal children disappeared, I feared something evil in the air. I first curried Bleakard's favor." All this the first head said. And when it took a breath to continue, the second head broke in.

"And when I had discovered who he really was, I denounced him to the king. But the king was so besotted with the mage, he dismissed me as two-faced. And Bleakard came to my chamber that very night," the second head said.

"And," the first inserted, finishing the story in a rush, "he said, 'Two-faced you are, then two-faced be.' He brought his magic flute down upon my head. I must have fainted, for when I awoke I was as you see me now. And that is all I remember."

Both heads turned and glared at one another for a moment, and then began to weep.

Jared, who had been shaking his head slowly from side to side during the dwarf's recital, suddenly spoke. "There is something familiar about your tale. And something familiar about your faces. But upon my very life, my head is a cloud and has been so since Bleakard enchanted me. I can think of nothing but my own sad fate. For look, friend, I too am cursed by that mage. So I have joined my young friend here to break the wizard as he has broken me."

"But do you dare to go to his castle?" asked the dwarf, the two heads again united in the question. "He would kill you, as he threatened me that night, with worse than death if I return."

"Could aught be worse than the way you are now?" asked Lann softly.

"Yes," said the one head.

"No," said the other.

"No," agreed the first.

"Yes," agreed the second.

And in the end, the two-headed dwarf joined the giant and the minstrel. As they left the meadow and entered the wood again, a wild goose and gander flew overhead in a direction opposite to that in which the friends were heading.

"Night is coming on," said Lann, as he remarked the birds' flight.

"How can you tell, with the sky so continually dark and the wood as black as a hole?" asked Coredderoc, both mouths working as one.

"Because the geese have flown home for their supper,"

said Lann. And then he told them of Bred and Bridda and Sianna of the Song. Both Coredderoc and Jared marveled at the tale and said it recalled something to them. But what it recalled, none of them was sure.

So arm in arm in arm, the three marched down the forest path. And it was only when Lann wanted to tune his lute again that the three friends dropped hands.

5. The Edge of the Cliff

Since it was indeed dark in the woods, whether day or night,
the three friends decided to push on. They sang with great
gusto. It was, Lann remarked, the first time he had ever
heard a trio that could sing in four parts.

They sang many of the old songs: "Hey to the Inn" and
"A Lover and His Lady Fair" and even "Lord Muskrat and
Black Elinor."

They sang some new songs, too. One was their special
favorite, which Lann had made up for the occasion.

> *"There once were three who would be four,*
> *With a hey, hi, ho and ho.*
> *There once were three who would be four,*
> *The tangled woods went to explore.*
> *With a hey and away went they.*
>
> *There once were four who would be three,*
> *With a hey, hi, ho and ho.*
> *There once were four who would be three*
> *A pestilence to wizardry,*
> *With a hey and away went they.*

There once were three who well-a-day,
With a hey, hi, ho and ho.
There once were three who well-a-day
A wicked wizard went to slay,
With a hey and away went they."

But as they got closer and closer to the end of the woods, the three friends with the four voices sang the last verse more and more quietly. Till at last they left off singing it altogether. "A pestilence to wizardry" was suddenly changed to "as penitants to wizardry." None of the three friends would lay claim to authorship of the new line. They didn't like it. It made no sense. But they found themselves singing it with quiet fervor as they drew closer to the wood's edge and the wizard.

Though the woods were beginning to thin out, it was difficult to notice it at first, for night had indeed fallen. Yet no stars lit their path. What moon there was, a pale, thin splinter, was shrouded with a gray blanket of cloud.

It was no wonder that they were practically at the edge of a cliff before they noticed they were out of the woods.

"The forest is behind us," said Jared with relief.

"The worst is ahead of us," said one of Coredderoc's heads. The other nodded in bitter agreement.

"Come," said Lann, "let us look around for a moment and then take turns standing watch. For sleep will be the Great Encourager. Only tired men are afraid."

"Then I must be perennially tired," muttered Jared, but softly so that only he himself heard it.

The dark was so deep that they could see nothing. The gray blanket never moved off the moon. The three friends huddled together for warmth. But warmth there was none.

Suddenly Lann remembered the feather inside his shirt. He took it out to see if there was some way he could share it with his friends. It felt unaccountably heavy, so he shook it. A down comforter sprang from the feather, soft and warm.

"Where does that come from?" asked Jared.

"From love," said Lann. Then he added, "Here, friends, and welcome. I will stand the first watch."

But first became last, for neither the giant nor the dwarf woke up until morning. Lann too fell asleep, his hand holding fast to his amulet.

When a wild goose and gander flew across the sky, they circled once around the sleeping friends, honking so loudly the three awoke at once. With great apologies to one another and waves for the departing birds, the three friends rose to greet the sun.

It was like no sun they had ever seen before. Instead of shedding a bright and cheery light, the sun looked thin and worn out, like an old penny. It hung forlornly over the edge of the cliff.

When Lann looked over the cliff's edge he shivered. There was no way down.

Yet there, in the middle of a lake that began at the cliff's bottom, was a huge crag of scaly gray-green rocks, and on the top, hunched like a vulture on dead meat, was a castle.

"Bleakard's castle," said Lann.

"How do you know?" asked his friends, though they knew in their hearts he was right.

Lann pointed.

Around the top of the castle, circling and circling and crying piteously into the wind were the wild goose and gander. Their cries carried clearly in the fetid air.

6. The Singing

"We must get down there and cross to the castle," cried Lann, his eyes still on the circling birds.

Just as he spoke, a dreadful sound rent the air. It was a high, sinuous piping that repeated and repeated the same seven notes. It insinuated itself into the air, and the repetitions seemed to engrave the evil melody on their minds.

"My head is cracking from that sound," said Jared.

"Your head!" cried Coredderoc. "Pity me. I have two."

"It must be Bleakard's tune. That infernal piping," shouted Lann above the noise. "How can one think above it?"

"Think we must," shouted one of Coredderoc's heads.

"Without thought, man is an animal," stated the other, and was immediately shushed by his friends.

"There is only one way to battle a spell of music," said Lann. "Or at least that is what my mother taught me."

"Well, hurry, whatever the way," said the giant with a shout. "My ears will turn to stone if I listen a moment more. All I can think of is that one hideous tune."

"Only music can defeat music," Lann shouted back. "And love, hate," he added in an undertone as if to remind himself.

He took his lute from the ground where it had lain all night. Without even stopping to tune, for tuning with that

177

constant piping was not possible, he began a song.

With their ears covered, the others could barely hear him. But if they could have listened with care, they would have heard the same seven notes of Bleakard's piping. But oh, the change! Lann's song took the seven notes and turned them inside out. He gentled them, calmed them, made them sing of love, not hate.

> *"My love is like a silver bird*
> *That flies to me when night is near.*
> *My love is like a silver bird,*
> *And oh, I wish my love were here.*
>
> *My love is like a silver boat*
> *That crests the currents of the air.*
> *And should I sink or should I float,*
> *It's oh, I wish my love were here.*
>
> *My love is like the fount of life*
> *That sprays into the summer air.*
> *My love is of my very life,*
> *And oh, I know my love is here."*

At first Lann's song was as gentle as lapping waves. But like the waves, his song was also persistent. And as the song continued, Lann's voice became stronger. The lute, which had sounded flat and brittle because it was untuned and playing against the strident piping, became richer and rounder and stronger, too. Till at last Lann's song filled the cliffside entirely, drowning out the grating flute. And when the three friends with the four voices finished singing the last chorus together, there was no pipe to be heard at all.

The moment the piping ended, the wild goose and gander stopped circling the castle. They hesitated for a moment in flight, and stood in the air like two figures in a tapestry.

Then, banking sharply to the right, they flew toward the cliff, their powerful wings beating in unison.

"We have won," shouted Jared, leaping into the air like a mighty fish out of the water. Where he leaped up, flowers sprang too. But when he came down on his left foot, flames shot out.

"We have just begun," said Lann. "For when one battles wizards, all things come in threes."

"Three?" asked the giant fearfully.

"Yes," replied Lann. "As my mother taught me—first the singing, then the seeming, and last the slaying. If there is any need for a last."

"What does that all mean?" asked Jared.

"I am not entirely sure," admitted the minstrel.

Jared shook his head and tried again. "What I mean is, are we the ones who do the slaying? Or are we the ones who are to be slain?"

"I don't know," replied Lann. "All I know is that my mother is always right."

"A pox on mothers who are always right," said the giant, and he turned away. "I think I will go back to my forest home."

"Stay, friend," said Lann. "Perhaps this time she is not right."

"I fear she *is* right again," said Coredderoc with one head. "I seem to recall such an unholy trinity."

"I *know* she is right," said the other head. "Look!"

The friends looked where he was pointing, at the crags beneath the castle. The very rocks seemed to unwind themselves and a giant gray-green serpent uncoiled and stretched, turning its ugly head in their direction.

As it uncurled, it moved its shoulders. Two giant wings began to unfurl.

"If that is a *seeming*," said the giant, "I do not like what it *seems* to be."

"What if it flys up to us here?" asked Coredderoc fearfully. "We have no weapons."

"Except my lute," said Lann.

"I fear that is not enough, friend," said Jared. "If that great scaly worm decides to fly here and have us for dinner, I fear it is not near enough. And as your revered mother has said, after the singing and the seeming comes the slaying. I fear, friends, we are all dead men."

Almost as if it heard the giant's voice, the great lizard pumped its mighty wings. The vast winds it created stirred the waters of the lake. And, with an awful scream, which sounded like the seven notes of Bleakard's song, the dragon flung itself into the air and plunged after the wild goose and gander that were fleeing toward the cliff.

7. The Seeming

As the great dragon came closer, the goose and gander, who had been flying wing to wing, suddenly parted. They circled separately to each side of the gray-green monster. Then each by each, they struck at the dragon's sides. The blows they gave it were but light little flecks. But like the kingbirds which can drive off the larger crows and hawks with many petty pecks, the goose and gander annoyed the monstrous worm. It stopped its headlong flight toward the cliff to try to strike its tiny tormentors.

The goose and gander flew out of range over and over again. When one was in danger, the other would swoop down upon the dragon. And in that way, the silver birds delayed the dragon's descent upon the three friends on the cliff.

"Quick," said Coredderoc, "I have a plan. I was a king's minister and I remember something of war."

"Tell us what to do," replied Lann, "and it will be done."

"First strip your lute of its strings," said the dwarf's first head.

"But it will never sing again," protested the minstrel.

"If you do not, *you* will never sing again," said the first head.

181

"Lutes can be replaced," said the other head. "But men cannot be."

"We are going to make ourselves some mighty bows," the first explained.

Jared slapped his thigh. "Well said, friend. King I may have been, but now I take your orders. Command me."

"Your part is next, friend giant," said the first head. "Gather all the sticks and twigs you can find and three large green boughs. Go to the right. I shall to the left."

Within moments they had a pile of wood. The giant was able to gather huge mounds of twigs and branches with his large hands. The three boughs they used as bows and strung them quickly with the lute strings.

"And now, friend, some fire. But just in the center of the pile."

With a wild bellow, Jared leaped into the pile of sticks. He hopped up and down on his left foot, and the pile burst into flames. The minute the fire was well begun, Jared leaped out again.

Then the three friends reached into the pile of sticks and, grasping the faggots by their cold ends, placed the flaming arrows into their makeshift bows.

"To me!" shouted both of Coredderoc's heads together as he sighted with his first head along the arrow shaft.

Jared and Lann took up the cry.

"To me!"

"To me!"

At their voices, both the goose and gander spun away from the dragon and fled to the cliff.

The dragon came after them straightaway.

The friends let go of their arrows at once. And though the bows were but poorly made and the arrows but poorly aimed, the dragon was such a large target they hit it with all three flames. Immediately the arrows struck, the three friends took up fresh ones.

The goose and gander dived down upon the flaming pile,

and each grasped a burning branch in its beak.

The gander raced toward the dragon's tail and scored the flame along its tender underside. But the goose, carrying a flame as large as her own body, flew straight toward the dragon's eyes.

When Lann saw where she was flying he dropped his bow. "Bridda, come back! Oh, come back!" he screamed.

But the silver bird never turned. At the last moment, when the dragon opened its mouth and it seemed certain it would swallow bird and brand and all, she dropped the flame into its mighty maw. At the same instant, she swept her wings to her side and plummeted straight down, down, down toward the lake.

Like a giant Roman candle, the dragon burst into bits of gray smoke and green flames, each part fell loudly into the lake with a hiss. A great cloud of steam rose to the clifftop, and for long moments nothing could be seen.

When at last it was clear, the three friends peered over the cliff's edge. They could see waves lapping at the bottom of the cliff over hundreds of broken gray-green rocks. And far out in the middle of the lake, a silver goose swam in ever-widening circles. Her feathers were singed, and the air was filled with the smell of burned flesh. But of the dragon, there was no trace at all.

8. Over the Perilous Lake

"So much for the seeming," said the giant.

"Do you think that also counts as the slaying?" asked one of Coredderoc's heads.

"I have not seen such a slaying in a long time," said the second head.

"But we did not slay anything," said Lann, strumming his fingers across the place where his lute strings had once been. "It *seemed* a dragon was upon us, but it was merely the gray-green rocks from the castle. Can't you see that?"

They all had to agree with him then. The slaying was yet to be.

"Now we must get off the cliff and to the castle," said Jared.

"Ah, but how?" asked Coredderoc's heads together.

"Not that I really want to go there, you understand," said Jared, "but I *do* have a plan. And if the rest is as simple as the first . . ."

"I hope the rest is simple, and it is not just we who are so," said Lann. "What is your plan, friend?"

"I will shake my right foot, and we will begin with many flowers."

"Flowers?" said the minstrel. "What good are flowers against a wizard?"

"Or lute strings against a dragon?" reminded Coredder-oc's two heads together.

"We must make a strong chain of them," said the giant. "Strong enough to carry our weight."

"Down the cliff?" asked the dwarf's first head. "But what good will that be?"

The second head added, "We would still need to cross the lake. And I for one—"

"For two," interrupted the first head, "can't swim."

"Not down the cliff," said Jared. "My plan does the two steps in one." He waved the gander to him.

The gander in turn called to the goose who swam in the lake, washing her poor singed feathers. The goose shook the water from her wings as she rose into the air. In moments, the two silver birds were on the cliff.

The gander walked right over to the royal giant. The goose stayed back, as if embarrassed to be seen. At that, Lann went up to the beautiful bird and caressed her head and looked deeply into her round black eyes.

"Fair heart," he said to the goose as if talking to a girl. "You have been most courageous. But there is more courage yet to be asked."

The goose dipped her head toward the ground, then looked up at Lann. The gander crowded close to him, too.

"You must carry us across the lake," said the giant. And then he described the flower rope that was to be built.

Swiftly, the three friends worked while the goose and gander cleaned their wings and made ready for the flight. Jared would stomp his right foot on the ground, and the harder he stomped, the larger the flowers. The larger the flowers, the stronger the stems. And the stronger the stems, the more sturdy and safe was the strand that they wove.

The giant's fingers were large and stubby, and he broke

more flowers than he could twist together. But the dwarf's fingers were quick and eager. And Lann's fingers, used to plucking a lute string, were the most facile of all. In less time than it takes to tell of it, they had twined a flower rope the length of three tall men.

"Now, I shall hang from one end, near the gander," said the giant. "And you, Coredderoc, and you, Lann, shall balance me on the other end, close to the goose."

The three friends helped the goose and gander slip the rope around their bodies like a halter. Then, positioning themselves as Jared had instructed, the giant, the dwarf, and the minstrel took hold of the rope. The goose and gander picked up the ends in their beaks.

"Hold fast, friends, and never lack courage," called out Jared, though he was the one who was most afraid.

The wild goose and gander began to pump their wings, up and down, up and down they beat together. Slowly the goose and then the gander rose in the air, the rope tight around their bodies, the ends in their beaks. And more slowly still, the rope stretched taut between the friends and pulled them into the air. As each one left the earth—first the dwarf, then Lann, and finally the giant—they said silent prayers for the safety of the others. And Lann said a special farewell to his mother.

Once fully in the air, though their burden was heavy, the goose and gander moved with ease. Their mighty wings beat steadily, silently, swiftly.

But the arms of the three friends were pulled nearly free of their sockets. And the three were soon weary beyond wondering.

Jared lost the grip of one hand less than halfway. Dangling dangerously and screaming mightily, the giant was borne through the air.

Coredderoc never said a word the entire trip across the lake. His two heads gazed soulfully at one another as if some important message were passing between the eyes of the two.

Lann, his unstrung lute across his back, crossed with his eyes closed the entire way. And whether he was singing to himself or praying, only the goose could have told, for she was the only one who might have heard.

But the rope stayed taut between them, and the goose and gander, bearing their heavy burden over the perilous lake, crossed the three friends to the castle that awaited them like a giant bird of prey.

9. The Slaying

The goose and gander lowered the rope with the three friends hanging from it to the crenelated castle wall.

The minute his feet touched the stones of the castle, Lann let go of the flower rope. He reached over to remove the halter from the goose's body.

After a moment, Jared did the same for the gander.

As for the dwarf, he knelt and kissed the stones with both his heads. Then he stroked the wall. "There is something familiar about this castle," said the first head.

"Yes, something like—yet not like," said the second head.

"It reminds me of my own castle," said Jared sadly. "But then, I suppose all castles are something alike."

Lann thought a bit. "It may be yet another seeming," he said.

"Is all wizardry seeming?" asked Jared.

"No, my friends," said a dark and sinuous voice. "The slaying is real. It is very real."

The three friends and the two birds turned slowly toward that voice, as if they did not want to know who had spoken. Or as if they knew and did not want to see. The goose began to weep real tears, which fell silently to the castle stones.

It was Bleakard. For so Jared and Coredderoc said together. But even if they had not, Lann would have known him. It could have been no other.

Bleakard was dressed in a long, billowing, blood-red robe. On his head was a crown of iron. On his fingers, dully gleaming, were iron rings. A large bone flute hung from a linked chain around his waist. His golden mustache and beard were streaked with gray and ran together down his face. His eyes were like two hollows and so deeply set that Lann thought he could see neither their color nor their size, though he knew they were black. And when Bleakard spoke, his words sounded like the hissing of a great snake.

Lann was afraid. But when he saw the goose weeping, every tear pushed him to action. "Hold, friend wizard," he said.

At that the wizard laughed. "I am no friend of yours, boy. But speak, as if words would help you. You are mine to do with as I will." As he spoke, Bleakard moved toward them. And though he raised neither his voice nor his hand, there was such menace in his every move that they all stepped backward until their backs crowded the wall.

Lann spoke then, braver than he felt. "Before every step there must be a chance," he said. "There was a chance for us before the singing. And a chance before the seeming ended. We *must* have a chance before the slaying. Magic is always fair. That I know, for so my mother taught me."

"*Feh!* What do mothers know of magic."

Lann looked calm. He even felt calm. He put his hand on his amulet and said, "My mother is Sianna of the Song. And all I know, she has taught me."

The wizard looked startled for a moment. Then the sneer crept back on his face. "And you think she has taught you well, young master? For if there is any who comes even near to me in magic, it is she, Sianna of the Song. But you are not she. No son is ever the same as his sire nor the equal to his dam."

Lann knew that so many words were meant to keep him from his purpose. So therefore he knew what his mother had taught him was right. For one who is assured of his purpose does not need words to spur him on. He took a step forward and said again, "What is our chance then, Bleakard? Tell us that we may at least try."

"You no longer call me friend?" the wizard asked.

"No, I now see you are no friend of mine, nor are ever likely to be."

"Well said. And truly said. I would be no friend to such weak, pitiful creatures as you. Hear me, then, Sianna's son. A single note is not a song. And you are not your mother. However, if you or one of your motley company will give up what is most precious to him, then you are all free. And I am slain. If not..." Bleakard lifted his right hand to his beard and stroked it slowly. "If not, you will join the gray-green rocks below. Alive, yet not alive. Slain, yet not quite dead. To come and to go at my call."

"What does he mean?" asked one of Coredderoc's heads.

"I am afraid I know," said the other.

"I mean...friends..." said Bleakard, "that you will *become* gray-green rocks, as have others who have incurred my wrath or displeasure."

The friends turned and looked down to the lake. Each felt he could see the shape of a man or woman in the rocks that lay broken and still in the water. As if in chorus, the three friends and two birds shuddered.

"Come, then," said Bleakard, "the little game begins. And what have you to offer—that which is most precious?"

"That is easy," said Lann, not daring to look at the goose as he said it. "Here is my lute. It is my most precious possession." He unslung the instrument from his back and handed it to the wizard.

"If it is easy," said the wizard, taking the lute and breaking it across his knee, "then it is not so important at all. A minstrel without a lute can still be a lover." He looked darkly and meaningfully at the goose, and swept the broken lute aside with his foot.

Lann looked down at the shards of his instrument. He felt doubly shamed. He had known that Bridda meant more to him than any lute. And so he had hoped to fool the magic, though he knew that magic does the fooling and is never fooled. He put his hand to his eyes and wept, and did not care who saw him weep.

"There, lad," said one of the dwarf's heads.

"There is yet a chance," said the other.

"Ah, what have we here?" asked the wizard with a laugh. "A two-faced friend. A counselor with no one to counsel? Well, counsel me. What have you to offer?"

The first head spoke softly, "Take my other head."

The second head snapped, "Wait, you can't give *me* away, I give *you* away."

"Both right and both wrong," sneered the wizard. He laughed louder still. "You cannot give someone else away. One person cannot own another. This game is funnier still."

Coredderoc's heads looked at one another. Then the eyes of the first head softened and the head spoke to its twin. "I am sorry. I mean it truly. You are precious to me. You *are* me."

The second replied, "It is true. We are both precious to each other."

The wizard fingered his bone flute with one hand and stroked his beard with the other. "Come now, I lose patience. You, giant, what have you to offer? Your marvelous feet?"

The giant looked down at his feet and shook his head miserably. He opened his mouth as if to speak, but fear closed it again.

The wizard smiled slowly and said, "And this is a company of friends. A fine rocky company you will make, too."

Lann looked around at his friends. He could scarcely see their faces in the gathering gloom. He realized that the sun had already gone down behind the cliff, as if to hide its face from what must surely happen to them in a moment. Darkness was fast coming on.

So Lann reached into his shirt and pulled out a silver button on a chain, the Magic Three. For the past seven years he had lived with it on his neck, and though often he had had a need to use its power, he had never tried its might. Briefly he remembered his mother's words those seven long years before. "Its consequences may be too hard to bear," she had said. Yet what could be worse than the certain living death of all his company? To lie forever by his beloved's side and be unable to reach out to her, a gray-green rock in a fog-bound pool? So he twisted it in his hand, first left, then right, then right again. And as he twisted it, he said the words "Magic Three of Magic Three, grant this boon I ask of thee."

From out of the darkened sky there came the sound of thunder. And the button twisted by itself in his hand.

> *"A precious gift give us to give,*
> *That all this company might live."*

Lann spoke the words in a whisper. There was another loud crash of thunder, and the magic button ran like quicksilver through his fingers and was gone.

Suddenly the two birds gave a moan and began to change. First the feathers on their heads turned to hair. Their faces changed from birds' to those Lann knew so well—his beloved Bridda and her brother. Then the feathers, soft and white on their wings, dissolved and the wings turned into arms.

Even before the change was complete, Bred moved over to his sister. He took her wing in his and placed it in Lann's hand. Then he knelt before the wizard.

"I give you what is most precious to me," he said.

"And what can be most precious to a man who is part bird?" mocked the wizard.

"I give you what is most precious to any—man or bird," said Bred. "For these my friends, I give you my life."

10. And After

The wizard still sneered. But deep in his hollow eyes, for the first time there was fear. It was fear born of certain knowledge.

Lann felt his heart contract with pain and relief. He felt ashamed of such a feeling and glanced at the others. He read the same thoughts in their eyes.

The wizard reached down for the bone flute that hung at his side. And while the horrified friends watched, the flute grew in size until it was as large as an ax and as sharp.

"*No!*" cried Lann. He leaped toward the wizard and Bred. But he was too late.

With a swift, vengeful movement, Bleakard brought the sharp edge of the flute down on Bred's bared neck. At the blow there was the red of blood and the black of night. And the entire castle moved as if shaken by an invisible hand.

When the darkness cleared, Lann looked around him in amazement. Of giant or dwarf, of goose or gander, of the wizard and his bone flute, there was no sign. The castle itself was changed. No longer were the rocks gray-green in color but a soft, warm brown. And instead of being on the cold tower walk, Lann was lying on a fair bed hung with velvet curtains.

Slowly he set his feet on the floor and got up. A small arched window beckoned to him. He walked over to it and peered out. Instead of night it was noon, and the sun's light was warm and full. The lake had disappeared and in its place was a great meadow with cows and sheep grazing and a company of herdsmen nearby.

Lann looked about him again, wondering if it had all been simply a seeming after all, a tale to while away an afternoon, a magic entertainment planned by his mother. But then, on a chest at the foot of the bed, he saw the pieces of his broken instrument. Picking the pieces up sadly, he shook his head. His life, he felt, was as broken as the lute. His friend's solitary death was, indeed, a consequence he could scarcely bear.

It was then Lann saw the open door. He went through it and found himself in a long hall hung with rich tapestries.

At the hall's end was yet another door. And when he opened it, Lann found himself in a large pleasant room filled with well-dressed people. As he walked through the door, the people all bowed.

"Hail, Lann, Sianna's son," they said at once.

Lann looked about him wonderingly and approached the people. For surely someone there could explain the things that had happened to him and help him find his company of friends.

Yet as he approached, the people fell back, bowing and opening up a pathway. At the end of the path was a throne. On the throne sat a kindly man who seemed tall as a giant, for he sat straight and proud. He was dressed in royal robes, yet beneath his golden crown was a face that was familiar.

"Jared!" cried Lann.

"It is indeed I," said Jared.

To his right stood a small man in robes of blue. A gold medallion hung around his neck. He was a counselor who looked at Lann with an expression he recognized at once.

"Coredderoc, too?" asked Lann.

"Cored one," said the counselor. "Both in one head."

Lann could contain himself no longer. He ran over to the two and threw his arms around them. There was a gasp from the people and Lann drew back, suddenly remembering that Jared was a king.

But the noise from the crowd was not for that. They were drawing apart to let a beautiful girl step through. Her hair was as soft as feathers and her face as gentle as the wind.

"This is my daughter," said the king, "whom I had thought lost forever. Bridda."

But Lann had not waited for her name. He had already gone to her side.

It was then that Cored explained what had occurred. "It was, as you have probably guessed, mostly *seeming*. We have all been enchanted, for our own folly or the follies of others. The king, the prince, the princess and I in our own sad states, in which you found us; the lords and ladies and cooks and stableboys as the gray-green rocks on which Bleakard's castle was built. For he was so evil, he could only build upon the wreckage of others' lives."

All the people gathered in the room nodded at this and whispered "How right" and "So true" each to his neighbor.

The king broke in then, saying, "We would have remained forever thus if you had not come by. With love and courage you inspired us to great deeds."

"But it was Bred who saved us all," protested Lann. "It was his sacrifice."

"Yes, in the end it was Bred, my son, who gave his life for us all," the king agreed. "Gave it without knowing who we all were—except that we were friends." He looked around at the assembly of people and then stood up. "Brave men do that, that others may live. And it will always be my special burden to know that at the moment of asking—

though I guessed what it was that was required of me—I could not do it. I was not as brave as my own son. That is a piece of knowledge that will guide me when I must judge others."

Lann turned to the princess. "But if you are of royal blood, then I fear what I hope for may not come to pass. For though there was never a one such as my mother, she is of the blood of peasants, and so am I."

"Lann, my friend, my son," said Jared, "you are ever as dear to me as the son I had for only a moment and lost. Marry my daughter and rule in my place. For any son of a woman as wise as Sianna of the Song is more than worthy to be a king. And Cored and I will serve as your counselors whenever such a need shall arise." And, taking the crown from his own head, he placed it on Lann's. Then Jared knelt before the minstrel-king. "Your servant and your friend till death," he said.

"May that be a good long time," said Lann.

"I sincerely hope so," replied Jared with such fervor that the two friends at last were able to smile.

So Lann and Bridda married with the blessings both of her father and of his mother, who came with her minstrel-husband to the wedding. The young king and queen shared in the ruling of the kingdom. Jared was ever at their side, leavening their judgments with his caution and wit. And Cored, too, served them well, as wise as two men, always seeing two sides of any question and balancing them both in any answer.

It was said that every night a silver bird with a blood-red ring around its neck visited the castle tower. King Lann played it songs on his lute. Queen Bridda fed it red berries, green salad, and wine. They called it Brother Gander and swore that it brought them news of all the people, great and small, who lived under their rule. Or so it was said in the kingdom—but many things are rumored, and not all are true.

What is true, though, is this: from that day on, no one within the kingdom was allowed to draw bow against any bird that flies in the sky or swims in the streams. And a flock of geese still lives contentedly in the palace courtyard, petted and beloved as any friend.

Here ends Book IV

ABOUT THE AUTHOR

JANE YOLEN is the author of many distinguished books for children, including *The Girl Who Cried Flowers, Neptune Rising, Commander Toad in Space, Dragon's Blood,* and *Tales of Wonder*. She has always been interested in folklore, fantasy, magic, and mythology, strands that are skillfully interwoven in *The Magic Three of Solatia*. A graduate of Smith College, where she now teaches, she worked for a time as a children's book editor for a New York publisher. With her husband and their three young children, Jane Yolen now lives in a lovely old farmhouse in Hatfield, Massachusetts.

ABOUT THE ARTIST

JULIA NOONAN's sensitive pencil and watercolor illustrations have appeared in many magazines as well as in books. An honors graduate of Pratt Institute of Art in 1968, she has already had some of her works exhibited at the Society of Illustrators show, and in the Children's Book Council showcase. She has "a particular interest in seeing that women in literature become *more* than decorative elements..." and especially liked *The Magic Three of Solatia* because of its attractive and adventurous heroine, Sianna. Ms. Noonan is a skilled enamelist and jewelrymaker, as well as a graphic artist, and also collects antique dolls as a hobby.

COLLECTIONS OF FANTASY AND SCIENCE FICTION